Praise for

SERVED COLD

*Winner of the Private Eye Writers
of America Shamus Award*

"TERRIFIC . . . written with intelligence and lots of humor. The political angle is unconventional, and potentially terrifying."

—*Friends of Mystery*

"The use of the Holocaust and its effect on survivors gives a sense of urgency to this debut detective novel. The historical background and the contemporary New York scene are both rendered excellently."

—Stan Johnson, English professor emeritus,
Portland State University

SERVED COLD

COLD

Ed Goldberg

BERKLEY PRIME CRIME, NEW YORK

SERVED COLD

A Berkley Prime Crime Book / published by arrangement with the author

PRINTING HISTORY
West Coast Crime trade edition / 1994
Berkley Prime Crime mass-market edition / August 1997

The Putnam Berkley World Wide Web site address is
http://www.berkley.com

ISBN: 0-425-15943-4

Berkley Prime Crime Books are published
by The Berkley Publishing Group,
200 Madison Avenue, New York, NY 10016.
The name BERKLEY PRIME CRIME and the BERKLEY PRIME CRIME
design are trademarks belonging to Berkley Publishing Corporation.

PRINTED IN THE UNITED STATES OF AMERICA

10 9 8 7 6 5 4 3 2

This book is dedicated to Adele Merchant. Without her love, support, and encouragement I would not have been able to produce it. I would also like to thank my friends, who have been kinder to me than anyone could reasonably expect. (You all know who you are.) And finally, I must mention my heroes from whom I have learned everything worth knowing: my mother Rose, my Uncle Murray, Lenny Bruce, and Gil Hodges. I couldn't have done it without you.

one

CHAPTER ONE. I AM BORN. Been used already? Well, I guess that these are the best of times and the worst of times.

This is all you need to know right now. I was born in New York City. Virtually from birth, I was immersed in the two activities that have stayed with me throughout my life: jazz and baseball. Regardless of whatever passions, long-term or of the moment, I have acquired, these two will always be my core of delights. In fact, if you add movies, food, reading, and sex, I'll be over in 20 minutes.

I was a conscientious objector during Vietnam, or at least I tried to be. ("Look what they did to Lew Ayres," my mother bawled. "Look what they did to Glenn Miller," I riposted.) Early in the war, they rewarded unpopular moral convictions by drafting you immediately and shipping you to a combat unit. My case was on appeal, and I was actually scheduled to be sent to 'Nam. In the nick of time, the courts permitted me to do non-combat service. I requested the medical corps. They made me an MP. So, I spent my service time policing drunk, stoned, and otherwise rowdy GIs in Germany and the Philippines. It was during this time that I learned about self-defense, weapons, police procedure, and a bit of karate from a deranged Okinawan fisherman whose near-lifeless body I pulled from a sump in Manila. He is a book in himself.

After I got out, I got myself together by hitch-hiking around upstate New York, New England, and Pennsylvania, watching minor-league ball in places like Scranton, Pawtucket, and Rochester. I read constantly, and pored through all of Sherlock Holmes and Raymond Chandler. I returned to the city, enrolled in a community college, and worked nights as a waiter.

I had a brief fling as a stand-up comic. This is the hardest job in the world, after things like brain surgeon. Think you're a funny guy? All your friends think so? Well, try getting up in front of a roomful of strangers who couldn't care less if you immolated yourself. If you aren't funny for three minutes with your buddies, no big deal. If you aren't funny for three minutes with the savages who frequent nightclubs, they throw furniture at you.

One night, at the restaurant where I worked, I got into a fistfight with an obnoxious customer and got canned. The next day I quit school, and on a whim, I applied for a Private Investigator's license. All that Raymond Chandler, don't you know.

I have an office in a quaking ruin of a building on East 14th Street, the northern border of hip squalor. North lies money and prestige. South lies tenements, hipsters, ethnics, and the yeast of urban ferment until you get to Wall Street, and the yuppie havens of Southport. I am certain that my landlady sneaks by the building every night to remove the "CONDEMNED" sign.

There are two floors of offices, four on each floor. Three are vacant. The offices sit atop a large store run by a Guatemalan refugee. The store is one of those places that has been going out of business for about six years. It sells everything from mattresses to plastic vomit.

The building also houses two lesbian psychics in separate offices. They fight each other for clientele every day, and sleep together every night. Talk about cozying up to the competition.

There is a marriage broker (Feinbaum's Love Link) in another office who has solved the problem of how to deal with baldness by painting the top of his head black. No kidding. When he takes off his glasses, you can see that he has painted the image of eyeglass frames on his face. I am waiting to see what happens if his nose falls off.

As a private investigator, most of my work is extremely boring. Sometimes, I simply go through court records, or real estate records for my clients. Other times, I stake out buildings and carefully note who enters and leaves. I get to serve a lot of court papers.

The work often involves providing bodyguards on an as-needed basis. I do most of this myself, but I have a list of dependable muscle I can use for the big or dangerous jobs. I am not a daredevil.

Sometimes, the work is spotty. I usually have a fund I can live off of during tough times, especially if I am frugal.

I won't take divorce cases. I know how messy they can be, and I am not the type to burst into motel rooms with Polaroid cameras. This cuts down my income considerably, but there have to be some standards, after all. Besides, the interesting cases make up for all the boredom and occasional lack of income.

two

THE EX-WIFE CAME BY the other day. It had been a while. I'll always love her for marrying me and for divorcing me when I needed it. The other day, I remembered why.

She was wearing one of her killer outfits from Bloomingdale's, or Neiman's or somewhere, that cost the equivalent of Mississippi's annual education budget. A tan suede skirt, tight at the hips and flaring, to accentuate her best feature and mask her worst. An electric blue silk blouse that picked up the eyeshadow over her tawny eyes, under a tweed jacket that got the eyes. Brown hair loose and flowing, parted in the middle. No other makeup but the eyeshadow. Her boots were glove-soft kidskin in dark brown, that clung to her chunky calves.

She was healthy, and rested, and the remains of a recent tan caressed her face. She looked just a few bucks short of a million, but in gold-standard dollars. Then, she opened her mouth.

"Christ, you look like an unmade bed."

"Dorothy Parker describing Maxwell Bodenheim. Unlike your current spate of boyfriends, I read books.

They move their lips watching television. You, on the other hand, look great, but beauty is as beauty does.''

"Fran Lebowitz. I guess I read the same books, and some people think I'm nice.''

"Some people think a man is made out of mud.''

"Tennessee Ernie Ford!'' we said at the same time, pointing at each other. We laughed.

"Seriously, Lenny, this place looks like you've been raising hogs. Why can't you get your act together?''

"Look, Sue, I'll always love you, and you are not wrong about this place. I'd like to tell you that I've had important things on my mind, but you wouldn't believe me. You've never understood why what I think is important is important. *Capice*?''

"Can you be a little vaguer than that? There was almost some information in that collection of random sounds. So, *bubbe*, what's on your tiny mind these days?''

"God, what a snotnose. If I hadn't gotten you out of your house, your father would eventually have flayed the flesh off you. I remember your shrieking matches with your sister. I can't remember what I found more impressive: your eternally fresh supply of creative obscenity, her psychological abuse, or that the sound of your voices caused every automatic garage door in the neighborhood to open.''

"My sister's mental apparatus qualifies as a blunt instrument.''

"Yeah, and I suppose calling someone a 'purulent vaginal discharge' qualifies as rapier-like wit. By the way, how is she doing?''

She sighed. "Her poor fucking schlump of a husband has to work his ass off while she refuses to work because she's an artist and must seek self-fulfillment humping her bi-sexual pottery instructor. He claims to be straight, but I doubt that he would have much luck keeping a rectal thermometer in place. What he sees in her is anybody's guess, unless it helps him appreciate men more.''

"Poor Artie. He was such a sweet kid when they got married. I guess nobody ever told him that you don't have to marry the first girl that you sleep with. So, what brings you here, anyway? Not that I'm not thrilled to see you.''

"Lenny, I'm frankly tired of seeing men for their genitalia alone. You really are a dear, and you always made me feel good in bed. Besides, no one amuses and provokes me like you, least of all the baloney ponies I've been screwing lately.''

"So, you're here because I've got a small dick and I inspire you to new peaks of sarcasm. Damn, you can turn a boy's head.''

"Don't be a schmuck. Take off my expensive clothes and make love with me.''

Afterward, we lounged in the rumpled bed, leisurely smoking grass and drinking cheap wine. She passed me the roach, and said, "My God, it's been a long time. Has your pecker always been that small?''

"No, I had cosmetic surgery. Have your legs always looked like a Chippendale sofa? All you need is a wooden ball under each foot.''

"Never mind my poor legs, you bastard. Didn't your mother teach you that it's not nice to make fun of the afflicted?''

"Maybe you can convince Jerry Lewis to run a telethon for your leg condition.''

"You weren't complaining a few minutes ago when

they were wrapped around your ears, mo-fo.''

"They say you are what you eat."

Sue groaned. "Of all the things you are, and their names are legion, a pussy is not one of them. I actually have some respect for you as a person. Shit, I'd worship the ground you walk on, if you lived in a better neighborhood.''

I snickered. "What have you been doing, taking holy communion at the Algonquin Hotel? You know, he said, musing aloud, I have often felt that you and I are out of synch with our time. We would have been far better off cracking wise with Benchley and Kauffman, and drinking ersatz scotch. No one appreciates this kind of stuff any more, and you are really funny and vicious. I like to think that I can keep up with you.''

"As long as we're high and speaking truth, I was just a small-timer until I met you. You showed me the value of a truly literate insult, and I never heard of Dorothy Parker and Anita Loos before I met you. My gratitude is eternal. Let's do it again. Maybe twice with a tool like yours is the ticket.''

Later, we went out for knishes at Yonah Shimmel's. We decided to see each other again. I knew it would likely not work out. But, she was fun, and she considered intercourse a creative outlet.

Besides, I will always love her.

three

I GUESS I SHOULD TELL you something about myself, but I don't like to talk about myself for several reasons, most of which I don't like to talk about. My personal history is hard enough for me to work through and make sense of. Trying to describe it is somewhat embarrassing for me, let alone to justify or rationalize it to strangers. On the other hand, I want to be a writer, and most of what I want to write about is based on my personal history. A conundrum, ness pah?

People call me Lenny Schneider. This is a lie. I find it easier to write about myself if I don't use my real name. So, I have appropriated Lenny Schneider. The really hip will know the significance of this name. It won't really matter for the rest. Call me Lenny Schneider.

You also know that I have an ex-wife named Sue, who is far too bright for her own good. She has educated herself beyond her capacity to understand. Books are not experience. Or, maybe she needs different books. She is probably reading deSade these days. God forbid she ever runs into Kraft-Ebbing.

We were married for a short time. I was young, she was younger. She once told me, "If we get married, we never have to worry about a date for New Year's Eve." Once she discovered that she was free from her parents, her siblings, and her responsibilities, freedom from me was next. She walked out on me the day before my 23rd birthday.

She has been in and out of my life ever since. Our relationship ebbs and flows with her moods, which are directly related to what she is reading and/or whom she is screwing. I shudder to recall her Khalil Gibran period and her biker phase. Most of all, I recall with terror that time she was reading H. P. Lovecraft and sleeping with a sometime off-Broadway actor who supported himself euthanizing stray animals for the city, and piqued his flagging lust with golden showers. Don't ask.

four

M<small>Y</small> LIGHT SCHEDULE
permitting, I decided to take a half-day, or so, and ankle
around the neighborhood. Years ago, I had moved to
that section of the lower east side which had been
dubbed the "East Village" by greedy real-estate types
to lure unsuspecting dolts yearning to breathe hip. My
own thought at the time was that the area was free of
the major worry of all New York neighborhoods: going
downhill. This place, a Major League slum, could never
get worse.

Who says I'm not naive? I never anticipated crack,
AIDS, Uzis, and the return of the fighting gangs.

The street I live on is roughly divided by a north-
south axis. East of this line is an established community
of Latinos, overcrowded and angry. West of the line is
a diminishing group of old-line residents, mostly Ukrainians, and a burgeoning of Asians of various nationalities
provoking the Ukis. Harmoniousness prevails amongst
the groups, as each hates the other passionately. Each
group is in complete agreement with the next about the
slanders repeated of the others.

The orientals eye me suspiciously. The Latinos eye me contemptuously. The Ukrainians avert their gazes, muttering ancient curses. The melting pot in action. Sometimes I think about moving to Iceland, where everyone looks alike, has the same names, and the only problems are vicious weather, alcoholism, and suicide.

I exited from my apartment building, looking left toward the East River, and right toward Avenue A. It was remarkably clear for a late morning in late summer, the greyish-brown miasma having retreated to about sixth-story level. Maybe it was the early morning rain that had made it so fresh. Whatever, it was a tonic for the soul.

I headed west, toward the subway, avoiding puddles as I went. I never step in puddles in New York. They are as likely to be piss or blood as water, and the water is nothing to trust.

Before I got a block, I was braced by a large man in a ragged suit. He was not quite the size of a Clydesdale. His nose was spread over his ruined pug's face. His single eyebrow was split by a fine, white scar. One ear was twice the minimum daily requirement of cauliflower, and the other was half-missing in action. If this guy's face were a road, 4-wheel drive couldn't hack it. I expected a panhandler. I didn't expect an expert blow to the solar plexus.

I can defend myself pretty well, and this galoot was not too fast. But the gut-punch winded me and hurt very effectively. So I back-pedaled, trying to retain my balance.

I found my feet, sucked in a painful breath, and smashed the son of a bitch as hard as I could in the middle of his chest. His piggy eyes widened, and he whooped in air. I knew I had slowed him down. I

reached into my pocket for a black-taped roll of nickels
I keep for these emergencies, and cocked my fist.

He lumbered toward me on instinct, and I caught him
flush on the flattened schnozz with a punch that started
somewhere in Canarsie. I saw his eyes go out of focus.
Then I saw a red flash and a number of stars as something heavy came down upon my head, like Maxwell's
silver hammer. I went down, not out, but not precisely
conscious either.

As I lay on the sidewalk, I dimly saw a greasy nerd,
horn-rim glasses held together at the bridge of the nose
by a flesh-colored band-aid. In his hand was the lid of
a steel 55-gallon drum, with a head-shaped dent in it.
He smiled a snaggly smile, and spat on me.

"You Jew fuck! You ruined my sister's life, and I'm
gonna ruin you."

Given my state of mind, I had no clue what he was
talking about. I sure didn't recognize him. He gave a
nod to his companion, and the thug started to kick the
living shit out of me. As I writhed this way and that, I
caught an occasional glimpse of my neighbors, who
were watching this with the detached air of olympic
judges. I expected them to hold up cards reading "9.6".

Greaseball began a clenched-teeth commentary as his
friend attempted to put me through the uprights. The gist
of it was that I had somehow developed evidence that
put his sister in the slam. That the client I did it for was
a fucking Jew bastard, and that I fit the description as
well. And that when his friend was finished I would be
eating gefilte fish through a tube for the rest of my pain-
wracked life.

Suddenly, a cop car careened around the corner, and

the two toughs took off through a nearby alley. This is one time I was happy to see the heat.

They checked me out, and called for an ambulance. I assured them that I had no idea who had done this, but it seemed to be a grudge.

The ambulance crew arrived, gave me a quick look-see in the vehicle, and decided that I was not damaged enough to waste more of their time, or a hospital bed.

The uniforms asked questions of my neighbors, none of whom had seen anything, natch. However, one elderly woman, the person who had called them, corroborated my account and description of the miscreants.

She was tired, she said, of the senseless violence. I told her that I was ill-disposed toward it my own self, more so of late. She said that she had been living in the area for 68 years, and that she was fed up. She was moving to Cleveland to live with her married daughter and son-in-law. I mused over our degraded era, when people move to Cleveland to improve their surroundings.

I thanked her profusely, assured her that I was alive only because of her kindness and public spirit, and lamented a situation that drove good people like her away. The crowd dispersed, the cops wrote down a few things and left, and the old woman shook her fist at the sky.

I spent the rest of the afternoon in Dirty Ernie's drinking draft ale. Since I had been battered, I reasoned, I might as well get fried. About three o'clock, I remembered a year-old job where I discovered that a mousy accountant was embezzling his boss blind, but was too clever to be detected. He was chipping on his mousier wife with a hot number whose demands can best be described as extravagant.

As it developed, the chippie was using the money that

Mousy gave her to support a coke habit, and a heroin habit for her horse-faced boyfriend, and her kid brother. Once the trail led to a junkie, a night in a cell without smack usually produced whatever data were needed. The boyfriend's face was not all that was horsy. A cop who strip-searched the creep swore to me that the guy's schlong was easy 15 inches limp. I couldn't remember anyone's name.

After another mug of Bass, I wondered if Sue knew Horsy. I was certain I had just made the acquaintance of the kid brother. After yet another ale, I slipped off the stool, and Ernie allowed as how I might want to go home and freshen up.

five

THE NEXT DAY, I SCHLEP-
ped to the office. I really didn't want to be there, feeling
a bit tender across my entire body, but Rifke ''Genghis''
Cohen, my landlady, would shortly be around for the
rent, and I was in my usual arrears. I was hoping that
some poor fool would require the services of a truly first-
rate investigator, but had stumbled into my office instead.

The concierge (really, the superintendent) had slipped
a note under my door informing me that a man named
Lou Goffin had stopped by yesterday while I was out
having my pummelling. He had been referred by Sister
Mary Louise. That woman would vouch for it if I
claimed I could walk on water, in spite of the fact that
the trick was registered in her boss's name. I must remember to send her a thank-you, and a bottle of Bordeaux. My number-one fun nun.

I called the answering service. A new guy whose
voice could remove barnacles informed me that I had
seven phone calls, three from Goffin, and four from

Genghis demanding the rent. This was serious. I called
Goffin.

"Thanks for calling back, Mr. Schneider. I really need
to see you."

"Can you give me some idea of the nature of your
problem?"

"It's better if I see you face to face. Should I come
over there?" He sounded upset.

"No, Mr. Goffin, I'll come to you. That way I don't
have to face my landlady."

Goffin gave me an address in the west 20s, over near
the Fashion Institute. As I headed for the stairs, I recognized the fell sloosh-sloosh of Rifke Cohen's dilapi-
dated house slippers dragging on the cheap linoleum.
Correcting my course 180 degrees, I made it to the fire
exit just as her stained housedress hove into view at the
corner of the hallway.

What would Raskolnikov do in a situation like this?
Nah. Out the fire door. Gone like a cool breeze.

six

GOFFIN WORKED IN A MIL-
linery factory. Ladies' hats, don't you know. This part
of the Garment Center had a bunch of hatmakers, and
was abutted by the wholesale flower district. In case you
think this is pleasant, you have never smelled unsold
flowers rotting on the streets by the metric ton.

Goffin's company was in a typical loft. It was old,
dirty, noisy with the sound of sewing machines and other
industrial clangor. The air was a potpourri of particles,
the healthiest of which was filth. The receptionist's cu-
bicle was glass on three sides and a desk in front. I
hoped the little Puerto Rican receptionist never had to
scratch herself or adjust her underwear.

She showed me to Goffin's desk, in one of a line of
offices surrounding the work floor, a chaos of machines,
wheeled bins, crates, and sweating humans of various
minority backgrounds. When we got to Goffin's office,
he was being harangued by a cliche fat, bald guy smoking a fat cigar. It must have been a good one, because
it stank like he was burning his socks. Cheap cigars all

smell good. Who says the poor have it rough? Anyway, I always found cigar smoking gross.

I cleared my throat. Fat Cigar gave me a look, and concluded his rant, obviously disturbed that he was unable to unfurl it to its full glory. When he turned on his heel, Goffin gave me a sick little smile and shrugged.

"Sorry, Mr. Schneider. Mr. Lefkowitz has been upset by my work lately. I'm afraid that my concentration hasn't been what it used to be."

"Ah, well," I said sympathetically, "we all get older."

"No, no. My mind's as sharp as it ever was, but I've been very distracted since. . . ." He looked around. "Come with me."

Goffin arose. He was a compact little man about 60, well dressed, but careless. His lunch, which was probably linguine marinara if his shirt and tie could be believed, was scattered on his clothing and exuded from his person.

He escorted me to a supply room, filled with what are called findings, little doo-dads like velvet bows and sequined what-nots that are stuck to hats. There were boxes and boxes of them stuffed into splintery wooden shelves. In the back of some shelves were ancient findings of great archeological significance, like if Alexander the Great had been a milliner he would have used them. They were at least six months old. God, the public is fickle.

Goffin interrupted this reverie by putting his garlicky mouth up to my ear, passing my unsuspecting nose in the process.

"Mr. Schneider, my uncle, Solomon Vishniac is, or could be, in a lot of trouble. Sister Mary Louise is an old, dear friend from Brooklyn, and she gave me your number.''

Goffin chuckled, and the vapors from his lunch changed the color of my tie. ''Yeah, I remember her from public school days, when she was Sheilah Rafferty. We graduated high school together. I had such a crush on her!''

He was right. Even umpty-ump years in the God biz had failed to wear away her Irish beauty and spitfire temper. Thank God she liked me.

''So Sheen, I mean the sister. . . .''

''Sheen?'' I interrupted.

''Yeah, like Sheena, Queen of the Jungle. That was her favorite comic strip. She even watched the TV show. She wanted to be Sheena.''

I made a mental note to bring this up the next time we got sloppy drunk together. I said, ''Forgive me, Mr. Goffin, but what does this have to do with Uncle Shloimy?''

He laughed. ''That's just what we call him, only not to his face. He's not a fun guy, as the kids say. My mother, may she rest in peace, remembered him as a killer-diller, always with the jokes. When he came here after the war, he was bitter and silent. My God, he was nearly dead.''

He leaned toward me conspiratorially, and I instinctively recoiled. He didn't notice.

''Mr. Schneider, I don't know if you are Jewish, but Uncle Solomon spent at least a year in Auschwitz concentration camp. You're aware that that changed people for good. My mother and her kid sister were sent here in the late 30s, just before it got really bad. Solomon and my grandparents stayed behind, not only because they didn't anticipate what was to come, but because there was a business to run, and Solomon was in university.

"Well, to make a long story short, Solomon watched the SS kill his whole family, father, mother, uncles, aunts, cousins. They dragged every Jew in the neighborhood out and lined them up outside the buildings. They ridiculed and abused them, especially the orthodox ones with the beards and *payess*, sidecurls. When the Nazis were finished humiliating them, they killed them on the spot. Shot in the street like dogs. Then they looted their houses. Solomon witnessed the whole thing. He escaped because he was returning from late classes and saw the carnage from a distance. He went underground, was shielded for a time by kindly gentiles, and was eventually betrayed to the Nazis by a neighbor. Those who helped him were sent to the camps with him. He survived the camp by killing his soul, becoming as hard as the Nazis, in his way.

"He's never talked much about his experience, and we never asked much. We do know that the people who hid him perished, as did almost everyone he knew. We also know that his special hatred was reserved for an Ernst Mueller and a Lev Kaminsky. Mueller was his barracks guard, and he performed acts I can't speak of. Kaminsky was a stool pigeon, and was eventually promoted to load and unload the crematoriums. For these, uh, services, he was rewarded with extra food and privileges. He survived. No, he thrived, because he was a failure and a bum before he went to the camps."

Goffin drew a crumpled handkerchief from a pants pocket, mopped his face, and loudly blew his nose.

"About six months ago, Solomon returned home from

an afternoon walk. He was white as a ghost. He fell into a chair, didn't even take off his coat. He sat for hours. Finally, he said one word: 'Mueller'.''

"Mr. Goffin," I inquired, "do you take this to mean that he saw Mueller? Here?"

"Well, Mr. Schneider, I can only tell you this. Since that time, my uncle is a changed man. He's in his seventies, and in good health, considering. Suddenly, he's obsessed with fitness. He walks for miles, he eats a special diet. My God, he joined a gym! For an old man, he's a *shtarker*, a strong man!"

"Well, look," I reasoned, "this can't hurt the old guy. It's given him something to do, something to live for."

"Well, young man, what you say is reasonable, and from an objective point of view would seem correct. But Uncle Solomon, well, you have to know him. One thing I would agree. He now has something to live for."

"What's that?"

"He's training like a fighter, like a Green Beret, and he's going to kill Mueller. This is his reason to live."

I looked into Goffin's face. It was the face of a man convinced that he was right. I was beginning to sweat in the close quarters, and Goffin's breath was making me swoon. The thought of Genghis Cohen was causing palpitations.

"Mr. Goffin, I'll take your case. I presume that you want Uncle Sol protected from himself. Just for the record, have you asked him again if killing Mueller is his plan, and has he denied it?"

"Yes, sir, Mr. Schneider. He hasn't even offered an explanation as to his health kick. He just tells me I'm wrong and to mind my own goddamn business. He talks like that.''

I wondered what poor Goffin would do if confronted by my ex-wife? I wondered what Mueller would do if confronted by my ex-wife? (''No, no! I confess to everything, only get her out of here!'')

''Mr. Goffin, my fee is $350 per day, plus expenses. Any unusual expenses will be cleared with you first. If the case appears to be taking more than a normal amount of time, we can talk about arranging something. Since my calendar is clear at the moment (the 'moment' being about two weeks, I thought), I can begin immediately.

''Oh, yeah. Now that I'm working for you, please call me Lenny.''

Goffin's worry-puckered face relaxed into a grin. ''Thanks, Lenny. Listen, are you married? What are you doing for dinner Friday? My Melanie is a great cook, and she's kept me alive since Sylvia passed away.''

''My friend, if you value our professional relationship, you'll keep me away from your poor daughter. If you want a character reference, I'll give you my ex-wife's phone number.''

''Lenny, Lenny. . . . Don't I know that there are two sides to every story? I won't ask what you can tell me about *her*.''

Baloney ponies stampeded through my mind.

''Seriously, Mr. Goffin, let me do some preliminary work on this, and I'll get back to you soon. Call me at once if Uncle Sol looks like he's about to go on a mission. By the way, what are my chances of speaking with him?''

''They would be much better, my boy, if he thought you were there to see Melanie.''

Somewhere, a trap went CLANG!

"Okay, okay, I know when I'm licked. What time is dinner, and what should I bring?"

I cashed Goffin's retainer check, walked to the landlady's apartment building, and slipped two month's rent, in cash, under Rifke's door in an envelope. Emanating from within, at ear-splitting volume, was Aaron Lebedeff's classic Yiddish song, "Rumenye, Rumenye." Anxious as I was not to see her, this is my favorite Yiddish tune, since my grandfather played it for me on his pennywhistle, singing the gleefully hysterical words (dancing! food! wine! sex! craziness!) between musical choruses.

To this day, nobody, not Armstrong or Bird or Bob Dylan, makes music as transcendent as grandpa playing "Rumenye, Rumenye" on a tin whistle. Ay, digga-digga-dom, digga-digga-dom. Hey!

seven

T HE NEXT MORNING, I called on Feeney the Weenie. Seamus Augustus Feeney, former professor of physics and computer science at the University of Minnesota, turned out of a job because of the Nixon recession, and his somewhat uncompromising southpaw politics. He returned to his native Manhattan to open, if that's the right word, a pushcart from which he sold the best franks in the city. An outrageous claim, but defensible.

Stately, plump Seamus Feeney sold his juicy, plump frankfurters a stone's throw from the New York Public Library on Fifth Avenue. "Feeney the Weenie" proclaimed his Kelly-green umbrella. Beyond that, the aroma of his wares, grilled or boiled, with your choice of onions, sauerkraut, two kinds of mustard, home-made chili, green tomato relish, cheese, or all of the above, was all the promotion he needed.

I met him at his office, on a beautiful late summer day.

"Schneider, the Hebrew gumshoe, the Shylock of

Sherlocks, the circumcised dick. What brings you to my emporium?''

"Fenian Feeney, with the Celtic weenie. The Hot Dog Hibernian. Greetings and begorrah, whatever the hell that means. I'd like one, grilled, with sauerkraut, Dijon mustard, and a dose of ipecac.''

"Coming up. Toast your bun?''

"You do, and I'll call a cop. Nyuk, nyuk. But seriously, folks, I came here for some professional advice.''

Feeney handed me one of his tubular masterpieces, suitably festooned with condiments. I attempted to discover an angle from which my lips and teeth could gain purchase. Shrugging, I simply tore into it, creating a colorful condiment cascade which terminated at my shoes.

Seamus looked concerned. "Careful, bucko, you're getting some of that in your mouth.''

He handed me a napkin. I ministered to my shoes, and got into it.

"Feeney, I know that you and your magic modem are plugged into every user network and bulletin board in the world. I need some information, and you are the man what can tell me. Is there, does there exist, an information bank on ex-Nazis, war criminals, their current whereabouts, etc.?''

Feeney put down his tongs and rubbed his chin. "Well, truth to tell, I have never needed anything like that, thank Jesus, but I believe it exists. What's the requirement here?''

"I don't know. It may be nothing more than a client's fantasy, but I'll need to check out some names. Can do?''

"Call me at home tonight, about eight. By that time I will have found it, or not. If I have found it, I'll run whatever names you have through the data base. If not, I'll let you know, and dig a bit deeper."

"Thanks, Feeney. What do I owe for this digestive terrorism?"

"It's on the house, bucko. You'll need the money for a shine."

I thanked him and left, hearing him break into Tom Lehrer's "Element Song" as I turned the corner.

eight

I STOPPED QUICKLY IN the library, leafed through some reference books, and put in a request slip for two books written about Nazi scum who came over here and went underground or assumed new identities. They were both out. The librarian told me that these kinds of books were frequently requested in this city of paranoia and long grudges. Even now, so long after the war, it was not unusual to see an older person whose forearm was disfigured with a concentration camp number tattoo.

As a kid in the late Forties, I had seen plenty of them. Most, young or old, were wraith-like, almost transparent, haunted. The only thing more hideous than seeing this tattoo was seeing it on a kid. None of the fat, comfortable American Jews could begin to understand them. They moved among us, and we reacted with awe and terror. Soon, to one degree or another, they adapted and we adapted to their presence. They were a constant reproach, and a lesson for us. They still are, or should be. When all of us who have actually known and spoken to, and been related to, the victims are dead, it is better than even money that the lesson will die with us.

nine

WHEN I GOT BACK TO
the office, I called the service. Goffin had called, so I
called him back.

"Lenny, so what's doing?"

"Well, Mr. Goffin, I have begun to do some research
into this case, and I hope for some results shortly. It is
very important that I talk to Uncle Sol."

"Ah. This leads to my second question. You're coming for dinner Friday?"

I gritted my teeth. "Yeah, sure. Is there any way we
could just arrange for me to talk to him? Without my
coming for dinner, I mean."

"Lenny, I promise you two things. One: Uncle Solomon will want to know what your business is. He will
be cagey and on his guard. We really need to have a,
what do you call it? A cover story. Two: You will not
regret it, *boychik*."

"Okay, Mr. Goffin," I said, suppressing a sigh, "give
me some directions. I'll be there with bells on."

I got home, avoiding a dogshit festival just at my

doorstep. This hound was part elephant, or was triplets. No dogshit in Reykjavik, I thought.

After a quick shower, I changed into my usual raggedy-ass clothes and went around the corner to Chen's for the best undiscovered Chinese food in the city. The black bean sauce alone is worth living in this hellhole to be near. A Tsingtao beer didn't hurt, either.

I wandered lonely as a cloud up Avenue B near Tompkins Square Park, stopping to admire the prodigies of weirdness arrayed in the streets. People used to think hippies were weird. We were like bank managers compared to these punks, queens, leather freaks, deinstitutionalized mental patients, and heavy metal kids. Everything just seems to have been ratcheted up on the bizarro scale. God knows where this will wind up in, say, 30 years. Perhaps there are the seeds of a reactionary not so deep inside me. I don't want to think about it.

ten

AT ABOUT 8:05, I RE-
turned to the pad and called Feeney. After our mutual
poetic abuse, we got down to business.

"Okay, Seamus, what have you got?"

"Ah, yes. There are several formal and informal bulletin boards containing just such information as you desire. I'm constantly amazed at what's available out there.

"The two that I focused on are best for different reasons. The first one is run by an obsessive in Milwaukee
who gets all available information from the obvious
sources, including all the famous Nazi hunters of Eu-
rope. You know, Wiesenthal, Klarsfeld, that bunch.
Also, he taps into a Justice Department source which is
not readily available to the outside world. The stuff is a
combination of well-documented info, mixed with raw,
unsifted reports.

"Next, there is Carl Dorfler. I met this guy at a con-
vention of bulletin-board users. He's as crazy as a bed-
bug. Only he's brilliant. His booth was rather, um,
flamboyant, what with the effigy of Hitler. So, I had to
check him out. After the usual techie blather, he told me

that his parents were German liberals who left as Adolph was rearing his ugly head. He is determined to track down the Nazi fugitives because he feels that they have tainted the Germans for all eternity. He wants to expunge them from the face of the planet.

"It's a crusade, bucko. The thing is, that he's in touch with operatives crazier than him. These guys claim to have actually tracked down some of the war criminals and assassinated them. They're hardly different from the damn Nazis."

"Well, okay Seamus. This sounds promising. Run Lev Kaminsky and Ernst Mueller against the data bases and see what we get."

I spelled the names for him, and we hung up. I found a San Miguel Pilsener in the fridge, and cranked up the CD player with Armstrong's Hot Fives and Sevens. I let Pops wash over me as I kicked back and sipped the beer. Just as I was about to light up a reefer, the phone rang.

"Yeah!" I bellowed into the mouthpiece.

"Me again," said Feeney. "I wish everything was this easy. The Mueller guy is reported to have entered the U.S. in 1946, with a new identity provided by OSS. He was considered valuable because of his intimate knowledge of the Eastern bloc. Before he was a death camp guard, he had been wounded on the eastern front. While doing his stretch at Auschwitz, he kept up with political and military developments through his contacts in the Wehrmacht and the SS officer corps.

"We have no knowledge of his current whereabouts, or his new identity. It's been changed at least once more since '46. Here's something that might interest you. His file has recently been activated by Dorfler because of an inquiry. It seems a sighting was reported here in the city. The organization is checking it out now.''

"What have you got on Kaminsky?''

"Well, now. Your Mr. Kaminsky is a piece of work, Leonard. Both data bases lit up when the name was entered. Current whereabouts blank. He arrived here in 1946 too, a war refugee, tattooed arm, the whole thing. He was arrested three or four times over the next couple of years for increasingly violent crimes against Jewish shopkeepers. The last robbery he apparently committed was a beaut. He pistol-whipped an elderly couple who ran a religious articles shop until their own relatives could not identify them. They both eventually died of their injuries.''

"Feeney, did you say 'apparently committed'?''

"Sure enough, bucko. The whole thing stank of his methods, but there were no witnesses, and he had an iron-clad alibi. A rabbi vouched for his whereabouts on the day the crime was committed. Ah, my friend, life is passing strange.''

There didn't seem to be anything I could add to this observation, so I thanked him and hung up. But not before I got the name and last-known address of Kaminsky and his alibi rabbi (ralibi?). One Rev. Maurice LeVine, of Park Slope in Brooklyn.

Rev. LeVine? Only in America would Rabbi Levine become Rev. LeVine. Even as an atheistic, assimilated, antireligious Jew, the stink of a self-loathing Jew turned my stomach. Einstein was right. We are not Jews because we say so, but because the world says so. We forget this at our peril.

A quick check of phone books yielded neither the

Kaminsky nor the LeVine. I brooded more on man's inhumanity, etc. Secure on my moral high ground, I smoked a joint and listened to Bessie Smith sing about careless love. I slept a troubled sleep.

eleven

THE MEETING WITH UN-
cle Sol was imminent and I wanted to have some mental
ducks in line before I went to speak with him. I called
a few of the rabbinical associations to check on the Rev.
LeVine. I got lucky on the third try when a Miss Bernstein, with a breathy girlish voice, told me the name
sounded familiar. She promised to get right on it.

For the next few hours, I busied myself with the paperwork that had piled up. Invoices from limousine services supplying bullet-proof cars. Private detective junk
mail, mostly slick brochures for exotic weapons and de-
vices. Real James Bond crap. Dunning notices to a major
network VP who had me follow one of his soap stars
for a week, until I saw the guy go into a gay bath house
on Ninth Avenue. The veep never paid up, and I heard
that the soap star's boyfriend, a network exec a bit
higher on the food chain, quashed the whole matter, apparently including my fee.

And so forth.

The phone rang. It was Miss Bernstein from the rabbinical association with news on LeVine. He was last

heard of as "spiritual director" of a holocaust survivors' center in Brooklyn, and seemed to have dropped from sight since. That was more than ten years ago. His file had a red flag.

"Mr Schneider, we only flag files for certain specific reasons. It's unfortunately true that the occasional, uh, turpitude mars the rabbinate. This man has two reasons for us to be concerned. First, his *bona fides* were never validated. What I mean is that we had to take his credentials on his personal say-so. He claimed that his records were destroyed by the Nazis when his seminary was burned to the ground.

"The rabbinical school he claimed was truly destroyed, and several other rabbis had the same problem. But, he never submitted himself to even the most casual verification of his status, and the investigator has added a personal note to the file expressing some doubt about his claim. Since he never took a congregation, the matter simply slid to the bottom of the pile."

As she spoke, a strange metallic clinking accompanied her voice over the phone line. At first, I thought it was line noise, all too common in some of the older parts of the city phone system. It was like the distant tinkle of elfin bells.

I asked for the investigator's name, only to be told that he had died many years ago. I asked for the second reason his file was flagged.

She cleared her throat, and the tinkling sounded. "This is hard for me to talk about. When he worked for the center, one of his duties was to counsel children of camp survivors in how to live with a parent, or parents, who had been through, you know, that situation. One of his girls was having a particularly bad time because her mother was losing her mind, and hallucinating about the camps. The girl was at a sensitive age, and couldn't cope. He used her vulnerability to get to her, and began a sexual relationship with her.''

She stopped. I could hear her gasping. ''Oh, God. Please give me a minute.''

After several seconds of no words and faint tinkling, she began again.

''Well, the mother found out. She caused a huge scene at the center, and demanded to see LeVine. She was shown to his office, and she screamed, 'My God, it's you!' and dropped dead on the floor. The girl committed suicide shortly thereafter, leaving a note confessing everything.

''It was at that point that LeVine disappeared.'' Tinkle.

''What does that mean, 'My God, it's you'?'' I asked.

''No one here had any idea. The guess was what you would expect, that she had met LeVine before, under bad circumstances. I don't know. Please excuse me, but this is terrible.''

Her emotional distress was communicating itself to me. I asked, ''Miss Bernstein, were you personally involved in this matter?''

''Oh, thank God, no! But this file is quite complete, and I've been looking through it as we speak. It has, I can't believe this, photocopies of the girl's suicide note, and a photograph of her body. She threw herself in front of a subway train. There is also a picture of LeVine.'' Tink-a-tink.

I was in a cab and at her office in 15 minutes.

The building was in the east 20s, not far from Gramercy Park, what was once a fashionable address, as recently as the 1950s. However, time and fashion had long since passed it by.

The lobby was dark wood and marble floors, with blue mirrors at either end, and some of the shrinks and financial advisors who populated the place in its hey-day were still hanging in. They probably serviced an elderly and diminishing clientele. The newer tenants seemed to be small technical firms, consultants, whatever.

What does a consultant do, anyway? Where is "What's My Line" when we really need it?

The rabbinical association was one of the oldest tenants, because the nameplate in the directory was old brass, one of about six left. A couple of the newer tenants actually had hand-scrawled paper nameplates, no doubt to give their clients a feeling of dignity and permanence.

I took the stairs to the third floor. The hallway was carpeted, and the walls had dark wood wainscoting, with a sort of pink/beige paint extending above. It was somber, dingy, and damp. I followed the signs to the office.

The door was one of those wood with pebbled-glass numbers with the tenant's name done up in block capital letters in black-bordered gold paint. I walked in.

The place was old and in slight disarray. There were four massive wooden desks on the right lined up along the wall with the windows, through which could be seen a brick wall about three feet away. I imagined that every year, on Rosh Hashanah at high noon, the sun actually shone into that space between the buildings. Of course, the office staff would not appreciate it, as they were at the temple. Or, they were doing what so many Jews in New York did on Rosh Hashanah: having lunch at a Chinese restaurant and going to the track or a ball game.

To the left of the door, all the available floorspace was taken up by old wooden file cabinets. Never mind the paperless office and the computer revolution. This was strictly a manila folder and typewriter operation. The two typewriters in evidence were vintage manual Smith-Coronas, each no larger than a washing machine and weighing less than a Buick. A really fast typist can make one sound like a Gatling gun, another machine of contemporary technology. One desk, second from the front, had a cardboard box on it for used carbon paper, with a hand-lettered sign urging that it be used again.

There was a plump, 35-ish woman at this desk, dressed in a dowdy, expensive grey suit, sensible shoes, and draped in gold jewelry. Her layered necklaces looked like chain mail, her bangle bracelets ran halfway up her right forearm, and a chunky gold link bracelet adorned her left wrist. She raised her hand to her face, and the bracelets went "tink-a-tinkle". She wore large, stone-encrusted rings on each finger except, significantly, the third finger of her left hand.

Her hairdo was a formidable helmet of lacquered impregnability, in a color which my ex-wife has dubbed "Hadassah red." Sue would have called her chubby face "as plain as a matzo-ball."

She was wearing huge eyeglasses, which magnified her brown eyes to the proportional dimensions of, say, a lemur, or some other exotic night-dweller. The glasses were the kind where the earpieces attach to the bottom of the lens. Her initials, GB in gold, were stuck to one corner of one of the lenses. This, and the fact that the other three people in the room were men, led me to deduce that she was Miss Bernstein.

I cleared my throat.

"Harrum. Uh, Miss Bernstein?"

She half-rose. "Mr. Schneider?" Her voice was even more little-girlish than it had been on the phone. She had calmed down some.

"Uh, yes. If I may, I would like to see the file on the Reverend LeVine."

The man at the front desk rose and walked over to me. He extended his hand. I shook it. He was a middle-aged man, balding, hair going iron-grey. He had a small mustache. His pudgy shape was encased in a glen plaid three-piece suit that would not have been out of place at the first Eisenhower inaugural. He held a burnt briar pipe in his left hand.

"Mr. Schneider," he said through a faint English accent, "I'm Hyman Zeldes, director of the association. That," he pointed to the man at the third desk, "is Hillel Bookbinder, and behind him is Murray Slotnick." Each in turn stood and bowed slightly. Bookbinder's hand-painted tie had come back into fashion. Never throw anything away, except clothing from the 70s. I nodded in acknowledgement. "You apparently have already spoken with Miss Bernstein." I nodded again. "We're compelled to ask your reasons for requesting this information. It's all very sensitive and confidential. Oh! Forgive me. Have a seat here by my desk. Coffee?"

I declined the coffee, and we both walked over to his desk. I sat in the guest chair, and he settled into his swivel chair, adjusting a red pillow at the small of his back. As he listened, he sucked absently at his empty, unlit pipe.

"Well," I began, "I'm in no way surprised that you're reluctant to show me the files. I would expect nothing less from so well-regarded an institution. How-

ever, I'm on the trail of Nazi war criminals for a private
client. This client has his own reasons for searching
them out, but the ultimate desired outcome is to expose
them and bring them to trial.'' Everyone leaned forward
simultaneously on his/her elbows, like a desk-bound drill
team. I went on.

"Rabbi LeVine supplied an alibi for a man accused
of a brutal crime, in which two elderly Jews were beaten
to death.'' Simultaneous gasps. "The man in question is
suspected of being a collaborator. Now, it's just possible
that everything is what? Kosher?'' Simultaneous chuck-
les. "But, we're checking just the same. I'd like to find,
and talk to, this LeVine.''

"You ain't the only one,'' Slotnick chimed in.

"Mr. Schneider,'' Zeldes said as he rubbed his chin,
"allow me to confer with my colleagues.''

They all congregated at the back desk, and went into
a huddle. Amidst much arm-waving, bracelet noise, and
whispered argument, punctuated by quick peeks in my
direction, they reached consensus.

Zeldes approached me. "Do you have any credentials?''

I showed him my PI license. He took it, squinted at
it, thrust it in the direction of the other three. They all
shrugged, in unison.

"Okay. Gertie, show Mr. Schneider the file.''

Miss Bernstein lifted a manila folder off her desk,
causing the gold hoops to slide toward her elbow with
a shimmering sound. There was a conspicuous red metal
flag affixed to it. She walked over and handed it to me.
The top item was a picture of LeVine, who looked about
twice as slick as he needed to be: well-barbered,
trimmed Van Dyke beard, tweed jacket.

Then there were various forms and official documents. A glance told me that they were of marginal value, because outdated. The aged and discolored photocopy of the girl's suicide note actually caused me to get lightheaded. I squirmed as I read the fading letters on the browning paper.

Zeldes turned to the others and said softly, "Aha. He's reading the note." They nodded.

Certain phrases stood out, as if in boldface, rendered even more agonizing in the careful girlish script, with little circles over the "i"'s instead of dots.

... I knew his kiss was not like it should be ... first he touched me in my private place and made me touch him on his ... he told me the pictures would be so he would always remember me ... I was scared and I tried to stop meeting him, but he said he would stop helping me and the other children ... he said that this was the way men and women made love and that I would never be a woman unless I did these things ... when I told Momma she got so sick and angry, I was so ashamed ... I don't want to live because I killed Momma and I am so dirty ...

The next thing in the folder was a news photo of her body, or what could be seen of it, lying alongside a subway car.

I fought faintness. When I regained some composure, I asked if anyone had known LeVine. No one in the office had been around long enough to remember him personally, but the stories about him were the kind that were passed down from staff to staff when the gang went out for beers, or whatever this crowd relaxed with. Seltzer, probably.

Murray Slotnick had the longest term of service, and

he remembered the investigator. "Yeah, I remember Irving talking about the case. He useta be a cop, Irving. Knew his stuff. He told me, 'Murray, this guy is a bad apple. You could smell him a mile away, this guy.' "

"Mr. Slotnick," I asked, "can you tell me any more about LeVine. I mean, what was he like?"

"Yeah. He talked with an accent, German, I don't know, and he had a camp tattoo on his arm. Irving saw. Also, Irving said he was a real big-shot type. Talked to other people like they was nothing, garbage. But, to Irving, he was smooth, high class, but sickening like— you know? The people who worked with him said he was a real smoothie when he had to be."

Slotnick paused for a moment. The only sound was Zeldes unconsciously sucking on his dry pipe. Bookbinder quietly sipped tea from a glass, a cube of sugar between his teeth, just like my grandmother used to do. Miss Bernstein looked on with a pathetic, agonized expression.

"Something else interesting," he continued. "LeVine worked with people who'd been in the camps. He was in the camps, but he never talked about his own time there. And when people spoke Yiddish to him, he refused to answer. He said, 'In America, speak English', but it was more like he didn't understand. A real snob."

I got up to leave. "Miss Bernstein, Mr. Zeldes, can I take this picture of LeVine?"

They looked at each other. "Sure," said Zeldes. "You want anything else? You want a copy of the note? We got a couple."

I shuddered. "No, thanks. I don't need to see that again as long as I live."

I was told that the holocaust center had been closed

down, more than likely because of the LeVine matter. No one in the office had a roster of the personnel, or could supply a lead to anyone who had worked with LeVine. Dead end.

I got up to leave, and shook hands all around. I promised to keep them apprised of any developments.

On the way back in the cab I ruminated, trying to keep my mind off the girl, her note, and the picture of her death. What, I thought, could make a presumably healthy woman croak in an instant? And what had she recognized in LeVine? The obvious thing would be something connected with the concentration camps. Maybe she had been in the same camp with LeVine, and being already emotionally disturbed, the sight of him was too much for her. Maybe she had been badly used by this guy, like her daughter had been.

I could speculate idly on this topic for ever. Idle speculation is my hobby, along with blasphemy and taxidermy. Take your goddamn speculations and stuff 'em.

twelve

AFTER THREE BEERS AT Dirty Ernie's, and another two at my apartment, I suffered a lapse of judgment and called Sue. She purred into the phone.

"Well, *tattele*, it's good to hear from you. I've been busting my ass working for the last couple of days, and I haven't had the time to be a bad girl. I think I'm ready for a break. Whaddaya say to a movie and a late dinner at Luna's? My treat."

"I guess," I replied cautiously, "if you want to see the double feature at my local itch. It's 'Where's Poppa?' and 'A Day at the Races'."

"Carl Reiner and the Marx Brothers. How predictable. Sure, that sounds good to me. I'll get in the shower and be down there in a half-hour."

Second-rate Marx Brothers is better than first-rate almost-anybody-else. Tootsi-frootsi ice cream, horse doctor jokes, and the serene, clueless Margaret Dumont. And, the Reiner movie, one of the rudest films ever made. ("Screw this up, Momma, and I'll punch your fucking heart out!") In spite of her attempt to be above it all, Sue laughed heartily and in all the right places.

Later, we grabbed a cab and went down to Little Italy. She endured once more my story of seeing Carlo Gambino in Umberto's, and we remarked on the encroachment of Chinatown into the Italian enclave. At Luna's, we had the mussels, canneloni, and braciola with linguine. Then, we scooted around the corner for espresso ices at Ferrara's.

We walked around Chinatown for a while talking about this and that, and then cabbed it up to her place so we could do it on clean sheets. Satin, at that.

After another bout of better-than-good sex, I talked to her about Uncle Sol, and Mr. Goffin, and LeVine. Not just to have something to talk about, but because she is smart and intuitive. Naturally, she smelled a rat with LeVine, but was unable to come up with anything but rank speculation.

So we did it again.

This was getting to be confusing. When our marriage broke up, she was up to here with my job, my aimless life, and our peculiar, increasing celibacy. (Our sex life had improved immeasurably after we split up.) She started screwing some guy she knew from work, and widening the emotional gulf between us. One night, she simply didn't come home. I didn't say anything.

The next time, she stayed away for two days. When she hauled it home, all I said was, "If you're going to stay out, at least call me so I won't worry about you."

She said, "Don't tell me how to run my life, you fuck!" The conversation became less elevated after that, and she was gone within a week.

Naturally, some of the blame for this is mine. I was blinded by love, and some stupid Hollywood version of "they lived happily ever after." I had seen a bad marriage up close, and I knew that *I* wasn't anything like that, so I assumed that nothing could go wrong. There were other problems, but I can't tell about them now.

Anyway, we were saved by hippiedom, and all its hedonistic, unbuttoned glory. War stories from the 60s are boring.

thirteen

THE NEXT MORNING, I
worried a bit about the dinner at Goffin's that evening.
I already knew what I would wear. I would try to be
casual/hip; myself, really. I had no idea what story Goffin would cook up to mask my true identity, so I decided
to let nature take its course. I set out khaki cotton slacks,
a pressed-but-weathered denim work shirt, and an old
and unstylish Harris tweed jacket that I have had for
years and love inordinately. Brown boots for my feet.
Middle-aged hippie clothes. Having assembled the outfit,
I stashed it in the closet for later.

I needed to do some shopping, and to think a bit about
the stuff swarming around in my head, so I hit the street.
I killed about three hours in all. Went over to the West
Village for some window shopping, and a wine shop that
I liked. I bought a bottle of St. Emilion, which I used
to drink a lot of, until I committed my life to beer. I still
drink wine, every now and then, but beer is food. The
latest in anthropological theory is that humans began to
cultivate grains so that they would always have something to make the beer with. We already know that yeast

for bread baking came from beer making. Beer is the staff of life.

Stopped into my favorite discount record store and bought a CD re-issue of some old Fletcher Henderson stuff. I resisted buying a CD player for a long time, assuming that the technology would follow 8-track tapes and quadraphonic stereo into Edsel Limbo. When it seemed destined to stay, I re-examined the possibilities. First, the re-issues of old and previously unavailable material, cleaned-up sonically and packaged well. Then, the crystalline sound, so refreshing to these jaded ears. When I heard 60s rock n' roll and 30s jazz like I never heard it before, I was hooked.

I ate lunch back on the east side at the Old Kiev, about which more later. Stopped into Dirty Ernie's for a beer, and listened to some lunching lawyers complain about how the area is going to the dogs. Ernie and I rolled our eyes at each other significantly. What was that Woody Guthrie line? "Some will rob you with a six-gun/ and some with a fountain pen." I counted the Mont Blancs at the lawyers' table.

When I got back to my street, there was a huge commotion at the building across and two doors down. It was a walk-up occupied by mostly Vietnamese and Cambodian immigrants. The cops pulled up just as I got to the place. I wormed my way up the stairs behind the cops, through a sea of horrified, chattering Asians.

An apartment door was opened just off the third-floor landing. The flat itself was furnished in old, well-kept pieces. One table and one chair were knocked awry. Between them lay the mutilated body of an old woman. In the corner a few feet away, stood a pit bull, jaws stained with blood. He seemed more frightened than anything, and actually wagged his tail when the cops came in.

The cops quickly confirmed that the woman was dead, although they summoned an ambulance as a matter of procedure. They also radioed for a dog-handling team. The dog seemed quite benign, but pit bulls don't have their reputation for nothing, and this one dripped gore.

Trying to keep my roast pork and red cabbage down, I angled as close as I could to see the victim. I could feel the blood drain from my head when I recognized the little old lady who had called the cops for me the other day. I remembered her vow to move to Cleveland. I wish she had done it.

I turned and left the apartment, and walked down past an old man on his way up. He was terrified, and uttered "Oy!" about every two seconds. When he got up to the apartment, I heard him lose it. I decided to wait outside until he came down. The fresh air did me some good.

The ambulance guys arrived, the same ones that had checked me out, and went through the crowd carrying a stretcher. About ten minutes later, they carried the old lady down in a body bag. The two cops half-guided, half-carried the old man down behind them. I waited until they had gotten what they needed, and he refused the ambulance guy's offer of treatment. I walked over to him.

"Excuse me, but my name is Lenny Schneider. Did you know that poor woman?"

"Oh my God! How could this happen? I went with her to get that damn dog. They said it was trained. Some training!"

The dog handlers arrived and headed into the building with various nets, boxes, and dart guns.

"You said you went with her to get the dog?"

"Sonny, you're a cop?"

"No, sir. But that lady may have saved my life the other day. She called the cops when I was getting beat up across the street."

"So, you're the guy! Alice told me about you. She said she wasn't gonna run away. She was gonna fight back, protect herself. So she got that *fahrcockteh hundt*! Oh, my God."

"Alice? Her name was Alice?"

"Yeah, Alice Costello. I met her at the Senior Center. She was a good friend, a terrific lady. I was sweet on her, and maybe we were getting together. Who knows? But, now. . . ."

The old man began to cry. I put down my packages, put my arm around him, and cried with him. I eventually collected myself enough to get the name of the guard dog seller, one K-9 Protex.

The dog handling team came down with the pit bull on a leash. No nets, no boxes, no tranquilizer darts. He jumped into their wagon like the family collie on the way to a picnic.

It was then I noticed that someone had stolen my CD and bottle of wine. This was shaping up to be quite a day, and it wasn't even two o'clock yet.

I walked the old man the few blocks home. He lived in one of those re-vamped apartment houses that appeared down here on the east side about 30 years ago. For some reason, it was believed that they would draw tenants here from other parts of the city. Modern buildings with lobbies and elevators and security, all the attractions of newer buildings elsewhere, and lower rents. That's nice, but you have to leave your apartment some time.

And the chances were better than good that some wino would be sprawled on the sidewalk in front of the building, or that you would be roughed up by tough kids. The poverty and despair were right there at your doorstep.

The Lower East Side has been romanticized in countless books and movies and biographies of vaudevillians who grew up here. The truth is that it was a slum then, and is a slum now.

We trudged the few blocks in a pained silence. Each of us had lost something that would not be easily replaced: he, the lover for his golden years; me, one of the last shreds of my hope for humanity. When we got to his building I asked him his name.

"Bloch, Herman Bloch. Thanks for seeing me here. I needed someone. . . ." He shifted uncomfortably, a bit embarrassed.

I fumbled for one of my business cards and handed it to him. "Mr. Bloch, if you need anything, I want you to call me. I'm serious. This has been a terrible shock to me, and I. . . ."

"A detective? You're a private eye?" He looked at me as though my card read "Martian" or "Sex Change."

"Uh, yes. I'm a detective. Is there something wrong?"

"No. I'm sorry. I just never . . . well, you don't look like a private eye."

This was not the time to crack wise. "I guess I don't. But, seriously, call me if you need anything."

He shook my hand. I watched him go into the lobby of his modern, secure castle. Safe from the barbarians in every way but the important ones. His defeat was written in his shuffling walk, and his burden plain on his bowed back.

I ran back over to the west side to replace the bottle of wine, and my Fletcher Henderson CD. I was so bummed out that I treated myself to a couple more discs. One of Thelonious Monk piano solos, and one of Country Joe and the Fish, their first album.

If I had seen this incident in the papers, or heard about it on the radio, my eyes would hardly have rested on it nor my brain fully registered it. It was just more static in the air of urban life. This bothered me, because every story like this happens to real people and has its costs, and the thickening of the callous over the thing that makes us human is not the smallest of them.

The rest of the afternoon passed in a brown study, a blue funk, or a black depression, given the moment. Life is so colorful here in New York, New York. The town so nice they named it twice.

fourteen

 T IME FOR THE SHOW-
down at the Goffin Corral. I got off the subway and
headed toward Ocean Parkway. My days of hanging out
in Brooklyn were long past, but the place seemed little
changed. The streets were trashier, and the buildings
grimier, but the large preponderance of Jews had given
way only slightly to inroads by other groups.

The old people still hung out on beach chairs arrayed
in front of their apartment buildings, or on the grassy
strip along the medians. The kids still played boxball or
Chinese handball—games unknown outside the New
York metropolitan area—or stickball, or jumped rope to
rhythmic nonsense words, or rode bikes at frantic speeds
on crowded sidewalks. You went out to shmooze, or
catch a breeze, or get a Good Humor, or escape the
reruns. Life went on in the streets, each neighborhood a
small town.

I stopped in front of the building. It was a pre-WWII
blond brick affair, built for the striving middle class. It
had a courtyard entrance whose granite paving stones
were obscured by chalkmarks, spilled liquids old and

new, and plain dirt. The remnants of what once were hedges grew in pathetic plots of soil along the sides of the courtyard. Trash collected among the foliage.

I stepped into the entrance foyer and read the names on the mailboxes. Goffin was in 4C, just as his directions, no more detailed than a manual on brain surgery, stated. The foyer was cool, slightly musty, and with an echo-ey quiet. I pressed the elevator button and listened to the ancient machinery shriek.

Under my arm was that pretty good bottle of Bordeaux, and a sixer of San Miguel. In my pocket was a picture of the divine LeVine. In my stomach was the dance of the polliwogs.

I got off the elevator on four, and walked toward apartment C. Food smells mingled with each other to make a surprisingly homey and delicious aroma. *Mezuzahs*, little boxes containing scripture, adorned each doorway. These are common on doorposts in New York. The *mezuzah* on C had been painted over about eight times.

When we were kids, we argued whether God lived in the *mezuzahs*. "God don't live in the *mezuzah*, putz. It's too small." "Oh yeah? God can live anywhere." "Okay, so how come he didn't come out when Artie lit the match under it?" I rang the bell.

Instantly, Goffin threw the door open. "I heard the elevator come up, Lenny. Come in. come in." I walked past Goffin into the narrow entrance hall. I passed the kitchen on my right, from which emanated sounds and smells, and continued into the dining room.

The rectangular room was well-worn and comfortable. The furniture was old, but good quality, and the walls had been painted an off-white in recent history. A worn rug covered the floor. An old, possibly European, sideboard took up most of one short wall. Opposite was a hodge-podge of framed family photos, apparently going back some time. Color snapshots sandwiched in plastic mingled with hand-tinted prints in elaborate mountings.

One long wall was bare. The other was broken by the entrance to the sunken living room, *tray chick* in the late 30s. The parquet floor was old and used, but well cared for. The living room was too dark to see into.

The table was covered with a starched, silk-trimmed tablecloth, and the best china was out. Someone had polished the silver. There were four places set, a wineglass in front of each, and a bottle of Manischewitz stood ready.

"I hope you don't mind, Mr. Goffin. I brought wine and some beer that I like." I proffered the wine store bag. He pulled out the bottle and his face broke into a huge grin.

"The good kind, boychik, with a cork." I smiled wanly. He disappeared into the kitchen and returned a moment later with the wine and the kind of corkscrew that comes attached to a can opener.

"Please. I have no idea how to do this." He placed them in my hands.

I took the bottle and the tool, and he vanished again. It was a struggle, but I got the cork out. He returned with an open bottle of beer and the glass that's left over from a *yahrzeit* candle, a memorial candle for the dead. We traded handsful.

He replaced the Manischewitz with the claret in the center of the table. I poured a glass of beer, and he motioned me to a seat at the table.

"Sit anywhere. No formality here." I sat, and sipped the beer.

"So, Lenny, I hope you like boiled brisket. We got fresh cornbread from Mastman's bakery, roasted potatoes, some vegetable: cauliflower or broccoli, the green one. Melanie insists that I eat less corned beef and more vegetables. Sylvia was from the old school, meat and potatoes. I actually took off a few pounds eating what Melanie feeds me."

Not because it was too vile to eat, I hoped. Actually, I loved boiled brisket. And, I hadn't had good cornbread in years. This is not the southern bread made from yellow cornmeal, but a loaf similar in appearance and flavor to rye bread, although tangier and denser.

"Mr. Goffin, may I speak here?"

He did one of those looking-around takes, and nodded conspiratorially.

"I've done some research into this case, and I have reason to believe that your Uncle Sol may have actually seen Mueller here in New York. Confirmation of sightings comes from a reliable source. Of course, assuming it actually was Mueller, we have no idea if he's still here, or what he's doing here. Yet."

Goffin's round face showed concern, and grief. "Lenny, boychik, I'm very impressed at your efficiency. But, my heart aches to know that this Mueller is at large. Not just because, excuse me, the son of a bitch doesn't deserve to live, but because my uncle might actually find him. God alone knows what'll happen, but it can't be good, no matter what."

I reached into my pocket and extracted the picture of LeVine. "Have you ever seen this man?" I asked. "This picture is a few years old by now."

Goffin studied the photo. "No. This man isn't familiar at all. What's his connection to all this?"

"At this point, I'm not sure. He may be connected to Kaminsky. Maybe he knows where Kaminsky is, if he's still alive." I returned the picture to my pocket.

Suddenly, Goffin switched gears. "Lenny, listen, here's your cover story. You're a fellow I met in the business, a findings salesman. I've invited you here to meet Melanie."

"How does Melanie feel about this?"

"Like you, maybe worse. She puts up with my little whims."

Our conversation stopped as the sound of the front door opening echoed in the entrance hall. "That will be Uncle Solomon. He's home from the gym."

A second later, Uncle Sol appeared in the dining room. He was dressed in a worn brown suit, scuffed shoes, a plaid shirt with black knit necktie, and a grey, stingy-brim hat. He carried a blue nylon gym bag bearing the exhortation, "Just Do It!"

His face had that translucent skin quality that old people sometimes get. His cheeks glowed, pink and healthy. His eyes betrayed nothing, except wariness. He put down the gym bag.

"So, Louis. This is the young man you brought for Melanie." This was stated flatly, as a matter of fact, in a breathy voice with a middle-European accent.

I rose and extended my hand. Goffin said, "Uncle Solomon Vishniac, this is Lenny Schneider. Lenny, my uncle."

The old man's grip was firm, strong. He did not feel it necessary to squeeze my hand to prove it.

"It's a pleasure, Mr. Vishniac. Mr. Goffin has told me a great deal about you."

Uncle Sol flashed Goffin a venomous look, recovered himself, and said, "Try not to let it give you a lousy opinion of me." I laughed briefly, until I realized that he said this utterly without humorous intent.

"Uh, have a glass of wine," I offered, "unless it's breaking training."

Sol looked at the bottle, and then over at my beer. "Mr. Schneider, if you brought this beer, which I see is not German, I'd rather have it."

Goffin leaped up from his seat and ran to the kitchen. Sol eyed me warily, but not with hostility. "When I was a young man, I enjoyed beer. The Germans made the best in the world. Since, ah, the war, I haven't had an appetite for anything German. Lately, I got a desire to drink a beer. But not German beer. This is from where?"

"The Philippines. I don't know how come so much good beer comes from the Pacific, but some would say that San Miguel is the best in the world. I like it, and I'm currently on a kick for it."

"Forgive an old man's bluntness, Mr. Schneider. I can't help feeling that your're here for more than a social call for my grand-niece. You don't look like a psychiatrist, but you might be a policeman."

"I assure you, Mr. Vishniac, that I'm neither." I tried to keep as blank an expression as possible.

"Maybe not, but you're no goddamn ribbon clerk, either."

Before I could respond, Goffin returned with a bottle of beer and another *yahrzeit* glass. I sighed a silent sigh. It was up, in terms of jig.

"*Nu*, Uncle Sol, you're suddenly a beer drinker.

You've become a constant surprise in your old age."
Goffin handed the beer and the glass to the old man.

"*Labele*, if I ever had a son, he couldn't be more dear
to me than you. But, you're full of shit, and a crummy
liar." Goffin flashed me a look that was half embarrassment, half I-told-you-so.

Uncle Sol went on. "I appreciate your concern on my
behalf. I know I caused you some bad moments lately.
Whatever the reason for Mr. Schneider's being in the
house tonight, he's not here for Melanie, and he's not
in millinery. He's here to spy on me?"

Much to my amazement, Goffin got angry red in the
face. "Yes, Uncle Sol, he *is* here to spy on you! I'm
tired of being treated like an idiot, and worrying myself
sick over you. I hired Lenny to make some, uh, inquir-
ies, to find out what the chances are that they'll find you
dead in an alley, God forbid, and that we'll have to go
to some morgue to identify you. I don't know what the
hell you think you're doing, but I wanna get to the bottom of this now!"

Now Uncle Sol got beet red, and started yelling at
Goffin in Yiddish, a language I understand slightly, but
not at that speed. Goffin gave as good as he got. Just
then, Melanie emerged from the kitchen, plates stacked
on her arms waitress-style.

"Shame on you!" she said. "Acting this way in front
of a guest. And on *Shabbas*!"

She was a big woman; no, sturdy is better, like an
athlete. She had red, wavy hair inadequately contained
in a hair ribbon. Wisps of it flew around her head like
solar prominences. Her eyes were a golden brown a few
shades darker than her hair. Her skin was fair and freck-
led, flushed with activity and embarrassment. She wore

a print blouse, unbuttoned far enough down to display freckles on a plump cleavage, and a denim skirt. Her bare legs were strong, and she wore beat-up Nikes on her feet. She was gorgeous.

On her left arm, she carried a large platter of boiled brisket, and a small one of horseradish perched above it. On her right arm were platters of mashed potatoes, green beans, and sliced tomatoes. The potatoes were that peculiar color indicating that they had been mashed with *schmaltz*.

The two men, chastened, fell silent. She stood, we sat, a tableau of indecision. I stood up, and said, "Hi, I'm Lenny. Can I help you with that?"

She blinked, as though I had addressed her in some unknown dialect.

"Uh, yes. Grab that horseradish before it falls in Pop's lap."

I took the small plate, placed it on the table, and relieved her of the brisket platter. She rearranged the plates and settings, and unloaded the other dishes.

She looked at me with a kind of mild shock. Softly, she said, "Uh, usually I have some chicken soup, but I couldn't find a decent chicken. . . ." Her voice trailed off.

Goffin leaped from his chair. "Lenny, my daughter, Melanie Adler. Melanie, this is my friend Lenny. He's a real cutie-pie, no?"

To my great relief, a wry smile worked over her mouth. "Yeah, Pop. Cute as a button. Hi, Lenny. When was the last time you were introduced like you were a ten-year-old girl?"

"Truthfully? Not since the time my drill sergeant escorted me to the debutante ball. He was like a mother to me, assuming that 'mother' is only half a word.''

The wry smile tweaked up a notch. Uncle Sol watched, impassive as an Easter Island statue, only his eyes moving slightly as though watching a miniature tennis match. Goffin beamed like a demented cherub.

Melanie said, ''OK, let's get this show on the road before it gets cold. I'll *bensch licht.*''

Goffin rose and moved to the sideboard. From a drawer he extracted three *yarmulkes* and an embroidered shawl. Melanie, meanwhile, set up two silver candlesticks, a *Shabbas* candle in each. Goffin handed the shawl to Melanie, and skullcaps to Uncle Sol and me, and put one on the back of his own head. I put mine on, and, with a mixture of guilt and delight, watched Melanie perform the ancient ritual.

Shabbas, the Sabbath, is personified as a queen who enters and graces the homes of Jews every Friday evening at sunset. It is the duty and privilege of the woman of the house to light the candles to welcome the queen.

I came from a house where this ritual was observed, in its beauty and awesomeness. When my widowed mother remarried, this ritual, along with several other of her finer instincts, was lost.

Melanie covered her head with the shawl. She lit the candles. Then she waved her hands over the candles several times and covered her face, as though capturing the warmth and light to herself. She whispered the accompanying prayer, as my grandmother and mother had done so long before.

Then, she turned with a smile and said, ''*Gut Shabbas!*''

Smiling, Goffin said, ''*Gut Shabbas*, Uncle Solomon, and to you, too, Lenny.''

I returned the salutation. Goffin said, "My Melanie has done this ever since her mother died. It is a tradition I would not, could not give up."

"I look forward to it," Melanie added. "It forms some kind of important continuity in my life."

"I told you, boychik. She's some girl, no?"

She was some girl, yes. "Yes, Mr. Goffin," I replied.

From there, the meal proceeded nicely. The food was delicious, the conversation light. Goffin actually seemed more intent on fixing Melanie up than on any investigation of Uncle Sol's activities.

Melanie bitched good naturedly about living with two *kvetches*. "They are always carping or grousing about something."

"Well," I said, "I guess you don't know whether they're fish or fowl."

Even Uncle Sol groaned. Melanie said, "I suppose it's superfluous to ask if you're a Groucho Marx fan."

"Who are you going to believe, me or your own eyes?"

"Oh, yeah?" she said. "Why I'd horsewhip you, if I had a horse."

As the wine and beer flowed, the mood mellowed. The excrement hit the ventilator over coffee.

Reluctant as I was to break the spell, I had serious reasons to be there. I fiddled with a piece of seven-layer cake, and cleared my throat. "Mr. Vishniac, I've enjoyed this meal immensely, but I've got a job to do."

The air in the room seemed to grow chilly, and Sol's face froze into a grim mask.

"First, I want to assure you that I'm not here to run your life. I hope to provide you with enough information so that you can either reconsider whatever plans you have, or make better plans. I have information that both Lev Kaminsky and Ernst Mueller have been seen in New York at various times since the war. There is a strong possibility that Mueller has been seen here recently. I want to stress that his presence is known to several groups whose agendas may be more, ah, forceful than yours.

"You might say they're planning the 'final solution' to the Mueller problem."

All eyes were on me. Goffin intent, Melanie with a level gaze. Sol said nothing, so I went on.

"A man in Chicago, who follows such things, has recently activated the Mueller file. I don't know why this could be so, other than for a very recent sighting. The Chicago guy's friends have been known to use this information to commit assassinations of former Nazis, here and in other parts of the world. If you are really planning to make a move against Mueller, there's a strong possibility that you may be caught in a crossfire, or some other unpleasant situation.

"Even if you're not directly involved in the matter, it's possible that your interest may have been noted by these goons. It might make for some legal problems. I doubt whether they would have the slightest compunction of trying to make you the fall guy here. To them, the end justifies the means. Now, where've you heard *that* before?"

The color began to leave Sol's face. He spoke coldly.

"Mr. Schneider, what you say is very interesting. I was honestly unaware of this. It might be good for me to reconsider."

A look of great relief passed over Goffin's face. Melanie's gaze swung over to Sol. Her expression did not change. Sol's eyes regained that opaqueness that indicated that he had cut off his inner self from the outside world. He was lying. I knew it, Melanie knew it. Poor, sweet, schmucky Goffin was the only one who was fooled. My guess was that he would immediately seek out these assassins, and try to use them for information.

Instant analysis: things were worse than when I walked in.

One more thing needed to be done. I reached into my pocket, and withdrew LeVine's photo. "Mr. Vishniac, do you have any idea who this man is?"

Sol took the photograph. He looked at it for a few seconds, crinkled his eyes, and stared deeply, as though his vision went far beyond the image. His face, at first just ghostly, turned a whiter shade of pale.

One whispered name. "Mueller."

Now everyone went pale. I could feel the blood drain from my own face. "Are you certain?" I asked.

He looked at me, through me. "He's had surgery. The nose is different, fleshier, and the jaw different. He had no beard. But I can never forget him, his eyes. This is Ernst Mueller. Where did you get this?"

I described my search, leaving out most of the important details. I made no mention of the sex crime or the mother's sudden death.

I indicated that the image was several years old. On an impulse, I related that he had provided an alibi to Lev Kaminsky to get him off the hook for the murder of two elderly Jews.

Sol's pallor disappeared in a flush. He ranted, half in Yiddish, half in English, with a soupcon of what I guessed was Polish. The gist was that the bastard son of a diseased whore was still working with that treacherous, hell-burnt, Jewish ass-licker to murder innocent people.

Melanie's jaw dropped, and Goffin broke a sweat on his face. Then, as quickly as it came, it went. Uncle Solomon calmly looked at me, and said, "Mr. Schneider, I'm pleased to meet you. I'm sure our Melanie found your visit stimulating. I know I have. And now, I must bid you all a good night." He bowed slightly. "By the way, thanks very much for the beer."

That brought me back from where my mind had drifted. "Uh, yes, well, you're welcome, I'm sure. I'll leave the rest of the six-pack for you."

With that, Uncle Solomon picked up his gym bag, and headed down the hall toward the bedrooms.

After a few moments, Goffin looked at me. "Boychik, I believe that we achieved some success here. Uncle Sol finally realizes that this thing is too big for him, wouldn't you say?"

"Sure." I stole a glance at Melanie, who gave me a slight nod.

"Well, then, send me a bill for your time. I appreciate your excellent work. I hope that the next time I see you here it will be for a, um, more pleasant purpose."

He grinned archly, and actually pinched my cheek. Melanie cracked up laughing. Between giggles, she managed, "I swear, if my father ever met the pope, he'd pinch his cheek!"

Goffin said, "Better I should meet Vanna White. Have I got a pinch for her!"

He then announced his bedtime, to leave us "young folks" alone. For the next few minutes, Melanie and I busied ourselves with gathering dishes, placing leftovers in plastic containers, and loading the dishwasher. By a great show of whining, I managed to indicate that I couldn't take all the leftovers home. We compromised on half the brisket, and about a half-dozen slices of corn bread. She made up a "CARE package" for me in a brown bag.

"Coffee?" she asked. "I've got real and unleaded."

"Ah, maybe half-and-half. I've got to stay awake for the subway ride, so no one slits my throat for the brisket."

We sat at the kitchen table, rather than returning to the dining room. The coffee was delicious. We talked about this and that. She told me to call her by her nickname "Mickey", earned because she hit like Mantle in sandlot ball games. She played stickball, softball, and would have gone out for little league, but her mother was afraid she'd get hit by a ball and made sterile, or something.

Even now, she played in an organized softball league. "I've lost a step, or two, so they put me on first. I like it. I'm in on almost every play. But, I'm really a shortstop at heart. When the Cards come to town, I go to see Ozzie Smith. Or Ripken, when the Orioles play here."

I asked her if she had ever been married. She flushed, and lowered her eyes. I apologized.

"No, no, it's a logical question. I was married for seven years, and I had a son."

"Had?"

"Yes. My husband and son were killed in an accident. My husband, Buddy, was a mate on a tugboat. He took Jeff out with him one Sunday to show him what goes on, on a tug. Just out here in the harbor. They were rammed by a boatload of escaping dope dealers, and everything went up in an explosion. They never knew what hit them.''

"My God, I remember reading about that. About two years ago?''

"Uh-huh. I'm just really getting over it. Pop wants me to 're-enter the land of the living', as he so delicately puts it. I guess I'm ready. I can't spend the rest of my life moping. What about you? You ever married?''

Somehow, the sordid story of Sue and me seemed like a petty follow-up. So, I merely mumbled, "Yeah, for about a year. It didn't work out. Maybe I'll tell you about it, some time.''

On an impulse, I asked, "Uh, listen, if you are free this Sunday, let's take in a Met game.''

She looked at me with narrowed eyes. "Are you doing this because of Pop?''

"No. I'm doing it because of you, and because of me. I like you, and I'm glad I had a chance to meet you, regardless of circumstances. Besides, it's not every day I meet someone who quotes Groucho Marx.''

"Okay, meet me tonight under the moon. You wear a necktie so I can tell you from the moon. One thing, though. This Sunday, I'm playing in a softball tournament. If we win in the morning, we play another game at 2 pm.''

"What time is the morning game, and where?''

She went through the details. Riverside Park, at 10 am. Thank heaven it wasn't in Brooklyn. What a drag taking the subway out there on a Sunday morning. I told her I would meet her there.

I made as if to leave. She went to the fridge and got

my bag of stuff. She handed it to me as I opened the door.

"Lenny," she whispered, "thanks for looking after Uncle Sol, and for being nice to Pop."

"G'night, Mickey. See you Sunday."

She gave me a kiss on the cheek. Even the ride home on the subway didn't spoil the buzz.

fifteen

I CALLED SUE THE NEXT morning to see if she wanted to go out for dinner, maybe go hear some jazz. I needed to talk to her about the Goffin case. I was determined to stick with the case until I felt that Uncle Sol was out of harm's way.

"Hello." I could just barely hear her above a din that sounded like salsa music.

"Sue? Lenny. What's the possibility of dinner tonight?"

"What? Is this Lenny?"

"Sue, could you turn down the music for a second? Christ, it sounds like Xavier Cugat on steroids."

"Hey, look, I can't hear you. Let me turn down the music."

"Yeah, yeah." I sighed, and waited for her return. In the background, the music dropped to the decibel level of a Concorde taking off.

"Lenny? Hi. Say, look, I really can't talk now. I'm packing for a little trip to Bimini with Raoul."

Raoul? Rah-fucking-ool? "Uh, Bimini with Raoul?"

"Yeah. I met him at Waldbaum's in the produce aisle.

We reached for the same guava. He used to be a Sandinista. Isn't that interesting?''

"Fascinating. You are going away with a Sandinista
after getting a grip on his guava. What else do you know
about him, besides the feel of his tropical fruit?''

"Here we go again, Lenny. I don't need you to run
my fucking life. I'm tired of your disapproval, not to
mention your sanctimoniousness.''

Not to mention my runt-of-the-litter genitalia.

"Okay, okay. I really needed to bounce some ideas
off you on a couple of things I've been working on.
Have a good time with Commander Zero.''

"Yeah, look. Something flashed on me when I was
running this stuff over in my mind. Don't ask me how
I came up with this, but. . . .''

The pause was excruciating.

"Well, goddamnit!''

"Yeah, well, have you ever considered the possibility
that LeVine may be Mueller?''

This woman never ceases to amaze me.

"What if I told you that you are absolutely right?''

"Motherfucker! I knew it! It was, uh, like a, like
something dropping from the ceiling. Like Newton's
fucking apple. How did you get this?''

"A positive ID from Uncle Sol. He saw the picture
and confirmed beyond doubt.''

"Oh, hey, I gotta go. That's Raoul at the door and
I'm not finished packing. Bye.'' Click.

The next time I hear some broad complaining about
men thinking with their groins, I will introduce her to
Sue. Raoul? I knew it would eventually come to a Raoul.
What's next? Horst? Guido? Mustafa?

Ah, fuck it. I gathered myself together, loaded Roland Kirk's "We Free Kings" into my Walkman, and took a stroll around Alphabet City. My head filled with manzello and strich.

sixteen

On the way home, I stopped at Licada's for a sausage sandwich. I had been patronizing Licada's since the 60s, when I didn't eat much for a while, and when I did, it was a slice of pizza and a hot sausage sandwich from Licada's. Their pizza was fairly typical of real New York Italian-made pizza: i.e., the best pizza in the world. The second-best pizza in the world is made by any other ethnic group in New York. There is no third best.

But their sausage sandwiches, well . . . Most sausage sandwiches are grilled, cooked on a hot sheet of metal, with onions and green peppers. You have your choice of hot sausage or sweet sausage, and each has its merits. Licada's, of course, goes this one better. They split the sausages and cook them over charcoal and dried grape vines on a barbecue grill. Unique, to my knowledge. The onions and peppers are cooked in the standard way, except for chopped garlic and fresh fennel added.

Also, the sausage is home-made in the basement by grandpa, who speaks almost no English and has the complexion of a jailbird. I think he only comes out of the dungeon to deliver fresh batches of the tubular ambrosia to a ravenous public. God alone knows what conditions or ingredients prevail in the manufacture of these gems.

Between Licada's and Feeney, the sausage requirement is nicely handled. I have heard tell of an old Pole in Bay Ridge who supposedly makes the best kielbasa and weisswurst in Christendom, but no one in the neighborhood has been able to keep a cat or dog for more than six months. I don't know about this one.

Hint for the novice: How to find a great sausage sandwich joint. First, all good sausage purveyors have a counter that opens to the street. Street trade is the first clue. Second, make sure that the sidewalk in front of the place is so greasy that it is difficult to walk or stand on it. This is the clue that they sell tons of sandwiches, the accumulation of dripped grease on the sidewalk. In the realm of great New York food, the voice of the *hoi polloi* is ignored to one's detriment.

And remember, always ask for well-done.

seventeen

M<small>Y</small> NUTRITIONAL AND exercise needs being satisfied, I wended my way home. As I turned the corner from Avenue A, I noticed a commotion of some kind in front of the apartment building where Mrs. Costello had been mauled.

What now? I went to look.

There was a rent-a-truck parked by the front door, and two burly guys carrying household goods down the stairs and into the truck. The commotion was a running argument between Mr. Bloch and a young woman I had not seen before. As I approached the building, Mr. Bloch waved me over.

"Mr. Schneider, come here. Maybe you can talk some sense into her." I groaned inwardly. "Mr. Schneider, this is Annemarie, Alice's daughter. She's convinced that something is missing from the apartment."

Annemarie was a trim, dark version of her mother, probably in her late 30s. Her straight black hair fell to her shoulders. Where her mother's eyes had been almost black, hers were a startling blue, striking against her dark features. She wore jeans and a Niagara Falls sweatshirt.

I held out my hand. "Hi, I'm Lenny Schneider. I'm very sorry about your mother. She was a lovely person, and a brave lady. Is there something wrong here?"

"Mr. Schneider is a private eye!" blurted Herman.

I smiled wanly. "Yes, but I'm just here as an interested neighbor. I'll certainly do anything I can to help."

Annemarie took a deep breath, and smiled. "Thanks, Mr. Schneider."

"Please, call me Lenny."

"Okay, Lenny. Maybe you can talk some sense into Herman, here. My mom told me about you the last time I spoke to her. This neighborhood sucks, and I tried to get her to move a million times. I was hoping she'd marry Herman and move out to the Island, or something. I know she was always threatening to go live in Cleveland, but she wouldn't leave New York for anything."

She paused, as if to collect her thoughts.

"Mom never had much of real value. She raised four kids on my father's salary as a bus driver, which is why we grew up in places like this. This place was actually a come-down from our apartment in the south Village, but she was born and raised around here, and she looked here when my father died, to save some money.

"Anyway, when my husband and I got a few bucks together, we bought her some things. We figured she deserved something, you know? At first it was small stuff, a little gold cross, a pair of earrings. On her sixtieth birthday, we got her an emerald necklace and matching emerald earrings, all platinum settings. Even with my husband's business connections, it set us back a bundle.

"Well, I've been looking around. I found everything but the box with the expensive jewelry in it. All the little stuff is there, even the dinky pearls. But not the emeralds.''

I asked, ''Are you sure she still had them?''

Bloch interjected, ''I never saw 'em. She never wore them with me.''

Annemarie smiled. ''Herman, you're a nice guy, but two things. First, you haven't known Momma that long. Second, you don't wear emeralds on pizza and bowling dates.'' Bloch flushed. ''My nephew Enzo is getting married in two months. You would have seen the jewelry then. We talked about putting the stuff in a safe deposit box, but she thought that would be a pain. She liked to look at them every now and then, and didn't want to have to go to the bank to do it.''

''Annemarie,'' I began, ''I was up in your mother's apartment very shortly after, uh, it happened. There was absolutely no sign of any rummaging around. The only mess was two pieces of furniture upset, probably when the dog attacked. If someone has stolen your mother's jewels, they knew just what and where to look.''

''That bothers me, too,'' she acknowledged. ''How the hell did they know where to look, and how come the goddamn dog didn't do anything? That beast was guaranteed to attack on command. Why didn't Momma have the dog attack whoever robbed her? What the hell went on here?'' She began to cry. Herman offered comfort. I offered advice.

''Have you reported the robbery to the cops? That would be the first thing to do.''

''No,'' she sniffled, dabbing her eyes with a tissue. ''Maybe one of the kids in the building . . . ?''

I shook my head. ''I don't think so. Would you enter a room with a pit bull with blood on his jaws? And still,

if you would, how would you know what to look for
once you went in? Nah. I doubt that anyone in *this* building went into that apartment.''

I gave Annemarie my card, and asked her to call me
to tell me what the cops said. I shook hands with Herman, and said goodbye to Annemarie, offering condo-
lences once more. I went across the street to my place.

Something about this matter was bugging me. It just
seemed too pat. There have been so many gruesome dog
attacks in recent years that it has become part of the
background noise of modern life. It could serve as a kind
of camouflage for something. You could cover a lot of
things with a brutal and spectacular dog attack.

And the devil-dog-du-jour aspect is intriguing. It's
like any other transient cultural phenomenon. Years ago,
it was German Shepherds. Then, Doberman pinschers.
Rottweilers were cheated out of their 15 minutes of fame
by the usurper pit bull. God knows what's next. Mas-
tiffs? Akitas? Jack Russell terriers?

Ah! Too much monkey business!

eighteen

AFTER A COLD BEER from the fridge, a quick look through *Downbeat*, and a listen to Jimmie Lunceford—"Jazznocracy" should be the national anthem, unless it's "Louie, Louie"—I walked up to my office on 14th Street to check the mail and my phone messages.

I wondered as I wandered, what was I going to do tonight? Sue was in Bimini doing the horizontal mambo with a guerrilla, I asked Mickey out for Sunday, and my latest squeeze offered to geld me if I showed up again. Touchy lady. As there were no other candidates, I decided to have a good, lonely-guy type of Saturday night: Chinese food, a movie, a session at Dirty Ernie's, either looking for unattached (not to say loose) females, or shooting the shit with the other losers.

Saturday night is the loneliest night of the week.

When I got to the office, the mail consisted of important personal messages ("You may already be a winner!"), bills, and a postcard from Weezil Furnham.

Weezil was a neighborhood pal who served in 'Nam, and then became a soldier of fortune. He was an idealist, basing his life on some Abraham Lincoln Brigade fantasy of fighting the forces of reaction. He was capable of, and had done, killing with his bare hands. After a while, he said that he could no longer tell the good guys from the bad guys, so he quit, lived off his considerable nest egg, gambled—usually successfully—from time to time, and traveled where whim and women took him.

His only stated goal was to have carnal knowledge of at least one woman of every race on earth. And they say that all the great quests have already been accomplished. His real name is Walter, but he is called Weezil because that is how he spelled "weasel" to lose the state semifinals for a national spelling bee. The word he had spelled just prior to weasel, was "glossolalia." Go figure.

Anyway, Weezil was now in Bali, getting a new slant on things.

The answering service had only one message, from Sister Mary Louise, wanting to know whether Lou Goffin had contacted me. I wondered what she was doing that night. Vespers, probably.

On an impulse, I called the Rabbinical Association. They were closed on Saturday, natch, which I would have realized if I had thought about it for a second. They did have an answering machine, no doubt of gentile persuasion. I left a message for Miss Bernstein to call me, that I had information she might want about LeVine.

I emptied the office trash in the hall incinerator, locked up, and went home. All the way home, I mulled dog attacks. When I got back to my apartment, I looked up K-9 Protex in the phone book. They were uptown, on 83rd. I called.

I presented myself as a potential client with several

business locations to be guarded. The cheerful female voice at their end of the phone informed me that their CEO, a Mr. Williams, handled commercial accounts. She told me he would be in Monday. I arranged to meet with Mr. Williams at 10 on Monday morning. I hung up the phone, and puttered around for a while.

Sue always hated my puttering around, especially just before bedtime. She saw it as a symptom of, an epitomization of, my whole existence. You know, shambling aimlessly around, idly performing pseudo-functions until I ran out of non-ideas, and then crashed.

Contemplating this short-circuited my puttering, so I took a nap.

nineteen

I WOKE UP ABOUT 7:30, tuned to the all-news radio station, and took a quick shower. The day's litany of grief went in one ear and out the other. The weather would begin to show the first encroachments of fall, with a clear, cool night forecasted.

I pulled on a pair of jeans, a long-sleeved T-shirt, and boots. I packed my large pocket knife, on an impulse. It is just barely legal, and can be opened with one hand. I added a leather jacket.

I went around the corner to my favorite neighborhood Chinese place. My mouth was watering in anticipation of mussels in ginger black bean sauce and a cold Tsing-tao. As I turned the corner, I was greeted by the astonishing sight of a huge crowd in front of the place. The longest I ever had to wait at this place was maybe ten minutes, if I hit the joint at prime time on Sunday afternoon.

But there was a line, a mob, for Chrissake.

If this weren't bad enough, a limo pulled up and disgorged Clyde Jamal, a star college basketball player who had just signed with the Knicks for some unreal amount. The kid would make more for one game than I ever did in my best year. What the hell was he doing here? In a limo yet.

Just then, Jimmy Chen, the owner's son and an old buddy from the hippie days, appeared to escort Jamal and his two (two!) gorgeous dates into the place. The crowd oohed and aahed and clapped. Jamal graciously waved.

"Jimmy! Jimmy!" I yelled. He spotted me and came over.

"What the fuck is going on here?"

"Shit, man, the dweeb who reviews restaurants for the *Times* gave this place a rave. It's been a fuckin' zoo for three days, and it shows no sign of stopping."

"What the hell was he doing down here? Isn't this a little off the Tribeca arugula trail?"

"Yeah, well, he got tired of free-range chicken and poached endive and decided to see how the real people lived. So, he's going into neighborhoods and fucking up your favorite local spots. You know. He gives a place a rave, and all the food-crit groupies turn the place into a living hell until he busts the next place. We'll get about two months of residual business, and then people will decide that it's just too much trouble to schlep down here for their mooshoo pork.

"Meanwhile, our regulars get pissed off, we have to hire staff that will get laid off when the fad dies, and our chef has threatened to quit six times."

"I thought your mom was the chef."

"She is. It's all empty threats, man, but you don't want to see your mom that pissed, believe me. Look, man, I gotta get back inside."

"Jimmy, please, can I get some mussels in ginger black bean sauce?"

"Yeah, hold on."

Jimmy looked into the front door, waved to catch somebody's attention, and shouted something in Cantonese. He turned back to me. "Wait a couple of minutes, Lenny. We'll get it to you."

"Thanks, Jimmy," I waved.

Jimmy pushed his way back into the place, advising his patrons to keep their shirts on. The crowd milled and swarmed like ants on a dropped popsicle. Old man Chen and Jimmy's brother Freddy held back the fleshtide with alternating promises of service and threats to haul out the cleaver.

The indigenous street people viewed the scene with horror, and rolled their eyes at each other in a "there goes the neighborhood" look. In the hierarchy of the east side, yuppies scored below junkies, and just barely above cops and Republicans.

Five minutes later, baby sister Tammy brought a bag out for me. She looked up at me through her large, round glasses. Long lashes framed her dark, almond eyes.

"Hi. Jimmy said it's on the house, and he threw in a cold beer also."

I smiled my best smile, reminding myself that not only was she the kid sister of a friend, she was 15 years old. I groaned inwardly.

"Thanks a lot, Tammy. See you soon."

She looked over her shoulder at the mob. "Yeah, maybe."

She pushed her way through to the door; my eyes drank her in until she vanished. Just as I turned to go, some rock star pulled up on a customized Harley. The girl riding behind him, her skinny and tattooed arms circling his waist, couldn't have been more than 14. I hoped he didn't see Tammy.

I walked back to the apartment, nose full of aroma of ginger, heart full of lust for Tammy Jailbait. I wondered how long it would be before I could have a leisurely meal at Chen's again, and watch Tammy stringing snow peas at a back table. I also wondered if Jimmy gave me a fortune cookie.

twenty

So, I TOOK IN A MOVIE, some serious, Eastern-European, angst-ridden nightmare about repression and the death of love. Just what I needed.

I cabbed it to Dirty Ernie's from the art house in the Village. I was tired, I was weary, I could sleep for a thousand years. When I got there, the old crowd was jammed into a corner, forced there by a plethora of recent neighborhood arrivals.

Well, okay. I am not xenophobic. Places have to change, or die. We needed fresh blood, and the new ones couldn't all be yuppie scum. But, the attraction at Ernie's was always the conversation, the quiet booths in the back where you could chat up a woman, dig the juke box, and sample the variety of draft beers.

The place was loud. The jukebox vainly offered the Three Sounds to compete with the talk noise. The back booths were full of laughing people slurping up pitchers of beer. The regulars drank sullen, ugly shots.

It didn't look good.

Ernie, and his wife and barmaid, Frieda, could barely

keep up with the requests for pitchers. Already, the Bass was tapped out, and the Harp was foaming.

I joined the old crowd, and drank Bushmill's. We muttered darkly. At 10:30, the place started to clear out. By 11:00, it was just us, drunk and nasty, and a ragged-out Frieda and Ernie.

"What are these," asked Phil Mooney, "fucking lemmings?"

"I wish," said Ernie. "Maybe they're all going down to the East River to jump in."

"The final insult to a once-pristine waterway," Mooney replied. He was a newspaper reporter, and our resident cynic.

We helped Frieda and Ernie to clear up the mess. He gave us all a round on the house, and closed up early.

I was sort of glad that it was still pretty early. I had to be dewy-eyed for Mickey on the morrow. I might have been up for hours arguing with old Mishkin about whether Kirby Puckett could have played with Musial and Mays, and why Wynton Marsalis was all technique and no soul.

I ambled the seven blocks home, trying not to think about Nazis or pit bulls. I thought about a skinny reefer and maybe a bad cable movie.

When I turned the corner from Avenue B, I spotted two shadowy figures, never a good thing in this part of town. It got worse. Despite the poor light, I was certain that this was the same little geek and his large friend who had crumpled me up a couple of days ago.

They had apparently come back to finish the job. They tried to melt into the shadows, but the big one was just too bulky for effective hiding, and the small one kept peering out to see the front of my building. Instinctively, I reached for my knife. Then, my brain kicked in: I got the hell out of there. It was time to find Bruno.

twenty-one

FINDING BRUNO IS HARD or easy depending on which part of his strange life he is into at any given time. Thankfully, he was in the third place I looked, a little piano bar on the cusp between east and west Villages.

Bruno is a better-than-average amateur jazz pianist. I first met him when he was playing in a now-defunct ice cream parlor on Second Avenue, about 1965. He was hard to miss, being 6'5" tall, and built like a pro tackle. His huge hands were surprisingly delicate, and he reached tenths on the keyboard quite easily. His main influences were pure New York: Fats Waller, Art Tatum, Thelonious Monk.

I made a point of speaking with him, and became not quite a friend, but more than a casual acquaintance. Our relationship had grown over the years, as our interests often overlapped. Bruno does not make his living playing piano. Bruno makes his living as hired muscle. He is a knee-breaker for local loansharks and revenge seekers, and does occasional work for mob types, but strictly on a contract basis.

He does not want to join any mob faction. He is respected for that, but lives on a razor's edge. A lot of people have scores to settle with him, and he lies low a good bit of the time. I have used him for bodyguard work.

Fortunately for me, he was playing tonight. I caught his eye as I entered the joint, and sat at the bar. He finished his set with Fats's "Jitterbug Waltz", and ambled over to the bar. He took my hand in his huge paw and shook it.

"How've you been?" he inquired. "How's Sue? I haven't seen the two of you in a long time."

A word about Bruno's speech. He has what most people would consider a terminal New York accent. It is almost incomprehensible if you have not grown up listening to it. What he actually said was "Haya ben? Haz Sue? I ain't seen da boda yiz sence God knows."

So, I traded quick amenities with Bruno and then cut to the chase.

"Listen, some slimeball has hired a thug to beat me up. They got to me a few days ago, and I saw them waiting for me in front of my place about 20 minutes ago. I think they mean to finish the job."

I described them. Bruno nodded his huge head.

"Yeah," he said, "I think I know the muscle. Probably Stash Kopetch. He's an old pug who's been doing this for years, since his ring career went into the toilet about 1955. Strictly small-time work. I never heard that he killed nobody."

"Well, old pal, I don't want to be the first. What's the chances of you coming home with me right now?"

"Lenny! This is so sudden. I didn't know you cared."

"Ha, wise guy. Seriously."

"Shit, yeah. This joint don't pay me nothin', anyhow. I could use a little workout before bed."

Bruno made his farewells to the owner, and we walked the few blocks back to my place. Kopetch—so ID'ed by Bruno—and the slimeball were still there. Bruno told me to walk up to my building entrance.

I hunched my shoulders, put my hands in my pockets, and made it up to my front step. A voice like screeching brakes reached my ears.

"Schneider, you cocksucker! You're dogmeat!"

The slimer held a kitchen knife with a ten-inch blade. Kopetch smacked a two-foot length of pipe into a gloved palm.

Given Bruno's presence, I went smart-ass to see if I could goad some information from them.

"Well, well. I bet you two girls have a beautiful step-sister named Cinderella back home. Hey, Kopetch. Too bad you didn't have a lead pipe when you were a stumblebum pug. You might've won a fight. What you really needed was a snorkel, so you could breathe on all your dives."

Kopetch actually growled, and made a menacing lurch, but slimer stopped him.

"Very funny, yid. Hotshot dick got our names. A real fuckin' Sherlock, hah?"

I took a wild guess. "Is your junkie sister and her horse-faced boyfriend on the street, or are they still in the slam with the rest of the vermin?"

A truly frightening grimace crossed his face.

"Motherfucker, you are gonna die slow. I'm gonna feed you your balls. My friend here is gonna break every bone in your fuckin' body, one at a time. Then I'm gonna feed you your nuts. I hope you're hungry, Jew-boy.''

"Why are you so hung up on my religion? Don't tell me you're a Nazi on top of your other obvious charms. What's your story, ratface?''

"My father raised me to hate Jew scum like you. He told me stories about how you poison everything, how you take food out of people's mouths. Everybody hates Jews, even the fuckin' Japs, and they ain't even got any there!''

"It's nice that you have such a fine relationship with your dad. Sounds like a peach. I guess, if everybody hates us, we must be doing something right. If you hate us, I know we're doing something right.''

"Enough bullshit. I'm gonna have Kopetch here start crunching you like a walnut.''

Now, I thought, would be a good time for Bruno to make his entrance. And, as the pug moved, so he did.

I don't know where he came out of, but he loomed behind Kopetch, and drove each of his huge fists side-ways into the guy's ears. Kopetch's chimes were rung, and he dropped the pipe. I, meanwhile, in no mood to be fancy, kicked the slimer square in the guts. He dropped the knife, and crumpled to the ground with a groan.

With amazing quickness, Bruno cuffed Kopetch's hands behind his back and threw me a second pair for the groaner. I cuffed him. The whole operation took about four seconds. It's great to work with a pro.

When Kopetch and slimer had recovered some, Bruno kneeled down and offered sage advice.

"Listen, you two weasel-dick bat-fuckers, Schneider is off limits, you dig? If I hear that he so much as got a bruise, I'll feed you to the fuckin' fish. Got that, Ko-petch?"

Kopetch grunted.

"You better stick to your dogshit, penny-ante stuff. Don't play with the big boys, like Schneider." He flashed me a wink.

"And you, worm-breath," he said to the slimer, "if you even think of gettin' even I'll personally pull you through your own asshole. What's your name, dick-face?"

Dickface moaned, "Nicky Carmine."

Bruno's face registered a funny, fleeting expression.

"Christ, are you Louie Carmine's fuckin' kid?"

Carmine grunted assent. Bruno gave me, what was for him, a pensive look.

He lifted both creeps off the ground by the handcuffs. Kopetch seemed to give him no more trouble than the undersized Carmine. He slammed them against the wall of my building.

"Okay, scram. I don't wanna see either of your dis-gustin' faces again."

"What about the fuckin' handcuffs?" Carmine whined.

"Get lost!" Bruno hissed, and kicked Carmine hard in the ass.

The two mugs ran down the street as fast as they could, and disappeared around the corner of Avenue A. I laughed at the sight, as much from relief as anything else, and turned to Bruno. His brow was furrowed, and he was not laughing.

"Uh, Lenny, listen. This Louie Carmine guy, the punk's father? He's bad fuckin' news. Even the mob guys are a little afraid of him. He's a psycho. Absolutely fearless. You could probably take him down yourself. Shit, he must be 65. But, you probably wouldn't be worth much for a while, and maybe never again.''

Bruno put his big hand on my shoulder. ''I once saw him take on a guy half his age. He was tough, but losin'. Then he bit the guy's throat out with his teeth. Carmine spat the guy's own blood back in his face, then gutted him with a straight razor while he was tryin' to stop his throat from bleedin'. Not a nice man.

''He also does horrible things to little girls. Runaways, kid hookers, whatever. He covers his tracks real good. Nobody can prove nothin'. But, we know he does it. He gives crooks a bad name. If sonny-boy goes cryin' to daddy, even *I* might not be able to help. Have a nice day.''

On that comforting note, he bid me goodnight and walked toward Avenue A, whistling ''Blue Monk.''

twenty-two

I WAS TOO WIRED UP TO
sleep, but I was supposed to be uptown at 10 to see
Mickey play ball. It was 2:20. Time flies when you're
having fun.

So, believe it or not, I straightened up the place,
loaded the dishwasher, changed the sheets (in case I got
lucky), showered and trimmed my beard, and crashed
about 3:30. I awoke at 9:30, threw some cold water on
my face, brushed my teeth, dressed hastily, stuck an old
Brooklyn Dodger cap over my messy hair, and cabbed
it up to Riverside Park.

I had the cabby stop at the Broadway Deli, and got a
toasted bagel with lox and a black Kona to go. We got
to the park at about 10:15. I walked into the park and
ambled over to a group who were obviously there for
softball.

Mickey was wearing sweat pants, a green T-shirt with
her team name (Nostrand Avenue Noshers), and an ad-
justable Mets cap with wild corkscrews of red hair stick-
ing out of the hole at the back. The rest of her hair was
mostly captured in an elastic. All around people were

warming up, playing catch, swinging bats. A couple of official-looking types were exchanging line-ups and discussing ground rules.

Circumambulating the group, I caught her eye. She flashed me a big, quick smile, and returned her interest to the goings-on. I sat on nearby bleachers and munched my bagel.

A tall black woman in a Noshers shirt was warming up her pitching arm. She windmilled each pitch, and zinged it to her catcher. Fast pitch; I said a silent "thanks." This eephus-lob, slow-pitch crap drives me nuts. I can't even figure out how to hit it.

The catcher was a stocky woman best described euphemistically as a "tomboy." She kept up a steady chatter of encouragement to the pitcher, whose name I guessed was Claudia. After a few minutes, she waved off another pitch.

"Save it for the game," she called, and the two walked over to the group, which broke up at just that moment. Mickey jogged over to me, with appealing movement rolling under her shirt.

"Hey, glad you could make it. You look tired."

I smiled wanly. "I had a late workout last night."

She cocked an eyebrow.

"No, it's not what you're thinking. More in the line of calisthenics."

"Well, whatever you call it, you need to get your sleep."

"I'll get plenty of sleep when I'm dead. What's happening?"

"Okay, it's like this. We play another Brooklyn team at 11. The Kings Highway Klowns. The winner of that game plays the Manhattan winner at two. If we can work it out, we will get a Bronx winner down here from Van Cortlandt Park at five. If not, the winner will meet them one night this week in Central Park.

"That'll be us, of course," she grinned.

"Jeez, isn't that a hell of a schedule?"

"Yeah, but the chances are good that the Bronx winner won't make it here. I assume that we can split about four."

"Do you think that we can contrive to have dinner, somewhere?"

"You bet! Can I shower at your place?"

Thank heaven I picked up the apartment. "Yowzah. Can I scrub your back?"

She made a face. "Pig," she said. Then, "Don't rush me."

"Okay, okay. Just a little joke. Can't blame a guy for trying."

With a wan smile, she turned back to the game. I finished the bagel, and sipped the coffee, kind of wishing I had another behind it.

The games set themselves up, and play began. I tried to keep an eye on both games with a preference for Mickey's match. I was trying to size up the opposition. The evenly matched Manhattan squads generally were not up to the Brooklyns. However, one woman on the Third Avenue Elevateds played shortstop like she was born to do it, hit solidly, and ran the bases with Pete Rose ferocity.

The little shortstop proved to be the margin for the Elevateds, who won 9-4. She drove in, or scored, eight of their runs. Their game ended well before Mickey's, which started out as a slugfest, and resolved itself into a pitcher's duel. With two innings left to play, the score was 12-11, and a tired Claudia was fighting to protect her one-run lead. The Elevateds came over to scope out the scene. I resisted the urge to chat up the shortstop.

When the Noshers came up in the top of the eighth, I walked over to Mickey. She was sweaty, and a patina of grime clung to her. She was drinking Evian water, and she offered me the bottle when I walked over. Lox-parched, I gratefully accepted.

"Are you enjoying the game?" she asked.

"Hey, it's great. Baseball is the best game ever invented. I wish I could be out there playing."

"Well, providing you don't blow your status with me, I could arrange for you to try out for next season."

"You know, I might take you up on that. The only problem I have, is I work odd hours."

"Hum, yeah. I forgot. I always assume that people have normal lives. Your life is probably far from normal."

I didn't want the conversation heading this way, at least not now. "Never mind that. The Third Avenue Elevateds won. They are not much, except for the shortstop. She's great."

She threw a glance at the woman, who was sucking down a Brooklyn Lager and laughing at a teammate's joke.

"Yeah. She's Bonnie Alper. The Manhattan teams are pretty lame, mostly, so she stands out."

"Don't underrate her. She's good."

"We won't have to worry about even playing against them if Claudia can't stop the Klowns."

"Yeah. She looks real tired, and her pitches are losing a lot of speed. Can she throw a backspin?"

"Gee, I don't know. She's always been such a power

pitcher. I guess she puts some English on the ball. I'll ask her. Hey, Claudia?''

Claudia ambled over. She was drinking a Diet Pepsi, and looked tired.

"Hey, Mickey, who's the hoodlum?"

"Jeez, does it show?" I laughed.

Mickey made the intros. Claudia sighed deeply. She said, "I guess I must be getting old. I ain't Old Rubberarm any more."

"Have you ever tried pitching with a backspin?" I asked.

"You mean to get them to hit grounders or pop-ups? No, I always burn them in. I've gone off the low end of the radar gun today, so let's talk."

Mickey and I showed her how to palm the ball so that it travels to the batter with a reverse spin. I said, "You can use the same motion as for your heater. Just try to keep it low. It's more effective that way."

"Don't worry," she replied. "I don't have the strength to pitch high."

The Noshers clawed out another run on the Klowns to make it 13-11. When the half-inning ended, Claudia threw me a wink and went out to the mound. She had trouble controlling the pitch, and walked the first two batters. Then, it clicked. The next batter swung early on it and sent a quick grounder to the third baseman, who stepped on third and commenced a triple play.

The Klowns were stunned, the Elevateds rolled their eyes. The fired-up Noshers scored six runs in the ninth, and the Klowns went meekly to their demise in the bottom of the inning.

Mickey ran over to me and gave me a big hug, and

planted a wet kiss on my mouth. Claudia ran over and said, ''Me, too?''

We clung together in a sweaty embrace, laughing and dancing like fools. There was about an hour before the next game, so some of the players took sandwich orders, and ran off to a nearby deli. We had about 35 minutes to eat by the time they got back.

The Elevateds had some time to rest. They hung back, and muttered darkly amongst themselves.

The next game was a breeze. Mickey, substituting for a tired Claudia, pitched well, mixing up a few heaters with some English to keep them off balance. Only Bonnie hit well, going four-for-five, but not scoring because of her team's nonfeasance. The Noshers won 6-1.

One of the umpires came over to announce that the Bronx would not, in fact, show up that day. The final match was scheduled for Central Park, next Sunday.

The thing broke up almost precisely on the dot of four o'clock. I asked Mickey, ''What's next, Killer?''

''Okay, let me get my gym bag with my change of clothes. We can go back to your place, shower, and then think about dinner.''

I nodded assent.

We cabbed it downtown. She looked around at my street, said, ''I've seen worse.'' She cooed at my apartment, which, while small, manages to be cramped.

She walked over to the rump-sprung couch and sat down. ''We have to talk.''

In my experience, these words have never preceded anything good. But, I was willing. ''Sure. What's on your mind?''

''Look, we just met, and I wasn't enthusiastic about it. My father means well, but you could have been one of the dorky dentists or divorced momma's boys that he has been parading before me for about a year.

"Obviously, you're nothing of the kind. You are the first man I've met that even interests me. But, Jeez Louise, I don't know anything about you except that you are Jewish and you have a weird, dangerous job. At least the dentists and accountants stand a good chance of coming home at night. I don't know about you. I've already lost one husband and family, and I figure his job was about one-quarter as dangerous as yours."

I made to protest.

"No, no. Don't interrupt me. Let me get this out. I know that even a CPA can get run over by a truck, or run into some punk with a gun. That's not the point. You gotta go with the percentages."

I let out a long sigh. "But, Mickey, I haven't asked you anything yet. I haven't made a single demand. Just a few, ah, flirtatious remarks."

"Yeah. I know. You don't have to. All this imaginary dialogue is going on in my head. I've composed a whole screenplay about us in the past few hours."

"What happens before we fade to black?"

"I'm not sure, but I've just rewritten this scene." She pulled me down to her, and kissed me deeply, her tongue searching my mouth. Our hands moved slowly over each other. She took my hand and gently placed it on her breast.

When we came up for air, she said, "Fuck it. I'm tired of being a good little girl. I don't know why, but I trust you. Let me take a shower."

She got up, grabbed her gym bag, and headed for the bathroom.

"There's towels in the closet just outside the bath-room," I called.

In a few minutes, I heard the shower start up, and then I heard her call out, "I thought you wanted to scrub my back."

Not too much later we made love. It gained in inten-sity as we went along and the weight of our respective individual baggage was discarded. Her body was athlet-ically fit, but soft with a ripe plumpness. She followed my leads and as her confidence and passion grew, led me to please her. We climaxed with a powerful physi-cality and a lot of noise.

Even if it never was this good again, this would al-ways be our magnetic north, our lodestar. We would strive to return.

Later, we took another quick shower and grabbed a bite at Licada's.

The rest of the evening was spent listening to Django Reinhardt and Stephane Grappelli, and renewing our commitment to life-affirming activity. Gypsy jazz and Jewish jazzing.

About 11 o'clock, I took her home on the subway. On the long ride back, I thought about what I thought. My love, she speaks softly. Valentines won't buy her.

twenty-three

MONDAY MORNING. NEVER my best time to begin with. The events of the past week, and my strange, busy, complicated weekend, left me even more muddled than usual. I showered, blasting jazz on the radio, dressed, and looked over the newspaper while having coffee.

My appointment with Mr. Williams at K-9 Protex was at 10, and I wanted to allow about an hour to get there, especially if I missed an express train. So, about 8:45, I began to rummage through my collection of business cards. I decided I would be Cliff Dennis, of Green Thumb Hydroponic Farm, a now-defunct business on Staten Island.

Not only do I never throw away a business card, I keep any I find, and I have even had several bogus ones printed for me by a guy I did a favor for once. They can come in handy when you have to establish a fast, but false ID.

I walked over to the Astor Place subway stop to begin the long journey uptown. I was dressed in my normal jeans and sport jacket, just what I suspected the hydroponic entrepreneur type would wear.

The office was in a storefront on East 83rd between a copy center and a laundromat, with venetian blinds going the length of the plate-glass front window. The K-9 Protex legend was painted on the glass, with a cartoon dog wearing a cop's cap. It was something like a German Shepherd.

I went in. The bare office was furnished in stuff that looked like it came from a second-hand motel furniture warehouse. The desk was one of those cheap, grey, metal things that showed all the dirt that it ever came in contact with. This one was no exception.

The desktop was littered with colored sheets from multi-part, no-carbon forms bearing the same legend and cartoon dog as the window. On the wall behind the desk, Polaroid photos showed the same paunchy, greying man in several situations featuring dogs, cops, civilians and guys in coveralls holding leashes. The dogs all looked like they should be wearing SS uniforms. There was a frosted-glass door to my right in the same wall.

The woman behind the desk was dressed in a double-knit pants suit like the ones sold in Sears, circa 1972. It was too small for her. Too small was the only size I had ever seen a double-knit suit come in. She smiled quite pleasantly at me and asked, "Yes, sir, can I help you?"

"Yes. I phoned here for an appointment to see Mr. Williams. I was told to come in at ten."

She consulted an appointment calendar. "Yes. You are Mr., ahh. . . ."

"Dennis, Cliff Dennis."

"Margo, that's the weekend girl, she has Lenny something. Shooter? That kid never gets anything right."

I clucked sympathetically.

She rose. "Please make yourself comfortable. I'll tell Mr. Williams that you are here. Coffee?"

"No, thanks. I've already had my limit today."

She smiled again, and knocked softly on the frosted-glass door. A voice from within bade her enter. She disappeared into the back office.

I sat on the genuine distressed naugahyde couch, and riffled through the magazines scattered on the wood-grain veneer table. There were old, well-thumbed *People* magazines, a *Time* with a cover depicting the world wearing bandages, a *Field and Stream*, which I hadn't seen since the last time I was in a real barber shop (I looked vainly for an *Argosy*), and a *Dog World*.

I picked up the dog magazine, and looked at the remarkable beasts pictured among the ads for dog food, flea dips, and exotic breeders. Some of these looked like Dr. Seuss animals. There was a cocker spaniel whose resemblance to any cocker *I* ever saw was limited to the general morphology (head, tail, legs, and so on). The dog's coat looked like a hairdo from a Ken Russell movie. The head and tail were merely suggested by protuberances at each end. I assumed that the photo was head on, but I would have declined to testify to that in court. The dog's name was Champion Paumanoke Chantelle Lollapalooza. A handle a stripper would kill for.

What name, I wondered, do they call her? Him?

My idle speculations were interrupted by the receptionist's return. She uncorked a dazzling smile.

"Mr. Williams will see you now."

I thanked her, and walked past her into the office. It was finished in imitation wood paneling, with a desk and chairs almost to match. Williams was the paunchy guy in the pictures. He had dozens more on the walls. In a frame was a picture of him shaking hands with Chuck Connors. In a frame next to that was picture of him shaking hands with Alfonse D'Amato. His desk was vacant, except for a wire sculpture of a golfer, a telephone, and a cardboard stand-up of the cartoon dog.

He rose to greet me.

"Mr. Dennis? I'm Dick Williams. Good to meet you."

"Dick, please call me Cliff, and likewise."

He shook my hand drily, firmly, and quickly. We sat down.

He diddled with the wire sculpture. "Mrs. Corcoran tells me that you are a commercial client?" he said, turning a statement into a question.

"Yes." I handed him my card. "I own several hydroponics outlets around the city, and I believe I need guard dogs."

He seemed puzzled. "What seems to be the problem?"

"Well, as I'm sure you're aware, hydroponics is about to go ballistic. People are increasingly concerned about what they eat, and worry about the contamination of foods via contaminated soils and water. We guarantee the freshest, safest produce in the New York area, and possibly the world."

His eyebrows went up, and he made a you-don't-say face.

"Competition," I went on, "is cut-throat. We've had three break-ins in our home research facility just to try to steal the culture medium we have developed for turnips." I paused significantly.

"Root crops, you can imagine, present a special challenge. We are about to deploy this new technology in our five retail centers, and we're concerned for our industrial security.''

Williams rubbed his chin. He looked me in the eye.

''As long as I've been in this business, I'm constantly learning things. Cliff, this is fascinating. What would you like us to do?''

I cleared my throat. ''Dick, the most feared dog in the world right now is the pit bull. I want a full-trained pit bull in each of my retail outlets, and three more for my research facility. Can do?''

Williams' brow furrowed. ''I was thinking more like Rottweiler, myself. They are more, ah, reliable in a role like this.''

''Don't get me wrong. I'd normally defer to your expertise in this situation, but my heart's set on pit bulls. Their deterrent effect is fantastic.''

He folded his hands and leaned toward me. ''Cliff, look, I'm gonna level with you. Only one guy on the whole east coast trains pit bulls for guard dog duty. He's out on Staten Island. He's flaky. A real weirdo. I'd feel much better supplying you with a more reliable dog, from a better trainer.''

I affected interest. ''No kiddin'. How weird is he?''

''Yeah, really,'' he laughed. ''How weird is he? I'll tell you how weird he is. He has attack-trained a Chihuahua.''

I blinked. ''Huh?''

''You know, a Mexican Hairless, one of those ugly little things that looks like it can't decide whether to be a rat or a dog. They weigh about half-a-pound, they're a few inches tall, and this maniac has attack-trained one.''

"What the hell for?" The mind reeled.

"Just to prove he could do it. This guy is nuts. The only reason we do business with him is because he's the only game in town. And, truthfully, we've been less than happy with his dogs."

"Dick, just out of curiosity, what's this guy's name."

"Ah, Rodriguez, Something Rodriguez. Ferdie, I think. He's a tough PR kid. Tattoos, big muscles, leather wrist bands, you know. We buy his dogs, and he introduces the dogs to the clients, takes them right to the house or shop, whatever. We pay him for the service. He at least is presentable to the clients. He doesn't show up wearing tank tops and boots."

"Dick, I want to think this over. I'm going to have to talk my partners into another choice."

"Okay, sure. If you want, I can give a little demo at your office, overhead slides and everything."

"A dog and pony show?"

"You're a real character, you know?"

We shook hands. I promised to call him. Liar, liar, pants on fire.

twenty-four

I TOOK THE SUBWAY downtown and headed for the office. When I called the answering service, the usual lady with the sweet voice told me that I had a call from an Annemarie Garfolo—whom I took to be Alice Costello's daughter—and one from Seamus Feeney.

When she finished reading the messages, we exchanged pleasantries. She told me she had been on vacation, and that her replacement was her boss' out-of-work brother. They had had several complaints about his lack of vocal finesse. I suggested that he might pursue a career making talking books for the profoundly deaf. She wondered how much he charged to drown out a symphony orchestra. I suggested a sliding scale from Mozart to Wagner. We amused ourselves no end. New Yorkers are so snotty.

I called Annemarie.

"Glad you could call back so quick," she began. "I called the cops and told them about the emeralds. They told me that a general-assignment detective would probably handle mom's, uh, case. . . . God, I can't say death. I still can't believe she's dead.''

She began to sob. I waited a few seconds.

''Annemarie, I'm sorry to put you through this. Did you ever get the name of the detective?''

She sniffed, blew her nose, and got herself together.

''Sorry. Okay, uh, here it is. I wrote it down. They called back with her name. Detective Jane Murphy. The original cops were Costa and Farnsworth.''

I wrote names on a scratch pad. I tapped the pen against my nose as I ran the names through my head.

''Yeah, I know the guys a little. They're good. I never met Murphy.''

''I don't know about a woman cop. What do you think?''

''I guess you're no feminist. Relax. Nobody gets a free ride in the NYPD, and I bet women have to be twice as good.''

I took down the phone numbers that the cops had given her. We signed off. She was still sniffling.

I called Feeney, but it was still during business hours, so I got his answering machine. After making a few rude noises with my mouth, I left a message. Maturity is a bore.

I called the cop-house, and spoke to Costa. He was an old-timer, smart and tough. But, all these guys are overwhelmed by sheer caseload. My cousin, who used to be an assistant DA in Manhattan, once told me, ''If you want to commit a murder, do it in New York. You get the first one free.'' And that was before the drug wars and crackheads.

I told Costa what I knew. I told him that I thought there might be an angle with the dog. He took the information down, making interested noises. He said he would pass it on to Murphy.

I asked him for a take on Murphy.

"Well, truthfully, we don't know her that well. She's new, but she's got a great rep. She transferred in from the Bronx."

"How is she personally?"

"You mean, like, what kind of person is she? She don't hang out in the locker room shooting the shit, so I dunno. She seems real serious, but somebody swears he saw her laugh at a joke. She hasn't got a partner, yet, so we got no info from that source."

"Okay. What have you got so far on the Costello thing?"

"Oh, Jeezis. We ain't got shit. I'd tell you if we had anything. The dog angle is the first hook we got, and it just came from you."

"Do you mind if I go talk to the dog trainer?"

"Does it matter? Just don't spook him. And don't let that fuckin' Chihuahua bite your pecker off."

"Thanks for the tip, Mr. Policeman."

Because of endless movies, books, and television shows, people have the idea that cops and PIs are natural enemies, like cobras and mongooses. Really, we generally get on well together, personalities aside, because we do a lot of the same work. We exchange information quite freely, except where the cops are constrained by the possibility of compromising the case, or where someone's privacy is at stake. Often, what a cop can't tell you is important. Mostly, it's not. Your reputation as an investigator can ride partially on how well you guess.

The phone rang. I guessed correctly that it was Miss Bernstein from the rabbinical association.

"Mr. Schneider? I have a message that you called."

"Miss Bernstein, the man you know as Reverend LeVine, or Rabbi, whatever, is Ernst Mueller. He was an SS officer who served at Auschwitz. His record, I'm told, is particularly brutal. Is there any way you can assure that he'll no longer be able to pass himself off as a rabbi?"

"Oh God, I wish there were. All we can do is distribute an alert to all the congregations in the area, and send it to other associations around the country. I don't think this has ever happened before."

"Do you need to have his picture back?"

"No, no. We've got another one. How could this happen, Mr. Schneider? How could a man like him . . . I mean. . . ."

I gave her a capsule version of how certain Nazis were slipped into the country because of their anti-communist value and their "unique" information, blah blah blah. I really could not answer her almost-unspoken question, and my explanation quickly ran out of conviction. I updated her on the plastic surgery evidenced in the photo, and promised to keep her posted on any further developments. We rang off.

Ruefully, I remembered Bob Dylan's "With God on Our Side." About how we forgave the Germans and made them our friends:

> "Though they murdered six million,
> In the ovens they fried,
> These Germans now too
> Have God on their side."

I'm really not into blaming the current generation for the sins of their forebears. But Mueller was just the kind Bobby was talking about. I went out to grab some lunch.

twenty-five

I GOT BACK TO THE OF-
fice just in time to catch the phone. Seamus Feeney
yelled in my ear.

"Lenny! Thank Christ it's you! Someone is after
me!"

I was not happy, nor very much surprised, to hear this.
I said, "Calm down, Seamus. Why don't you tell me
what's going on."

"Well, last night I was on the network keepin' in
touch with my various interests. On a whim, I tapped
into the Dorfler anti-Nazi bulletin board. When I ID'd,
my screen showed a message that I was to stay out of
things that don't concern me, and I was kicked out. Suddenly, my computer lit up like a disco. The anti-virus
program detected a killer virus that was trying to eat my
hard disk. Serious shit. Fortunately, the virus program
detected it. Unfortunately, this was a new type that the
program couldn't combat."

He took a deep breath. "Easy, Seamus," I cooed.
"You're hyperventilating."

"Christ on a crutch. Wait a second. Whew! Okay. So,

I powered down and rebooted off a floppy disk to min-
imize damage. Luckily, I had just backed up the whole
system, so I lost almost no data, but I was up all night
assessing the damage, reformatting the disk, and re-
installing software. My bookkeeping system actually
managed to copy the virus, and it's a stone motherfucker. The guy that developed this virus was not some
college-kid hacker. This thing is a goddamn weapon!''

"Seamus, I certainly apologize for putting your brain-
child in harm's way, but, except for some lost sleep,
what's the problem?"

"The problem, bucko, is that two nefarious types approached my wagon today and repeated the warning, and
stressed that what happened to my computer could be
as easily accomplished on my brain tissue."

"Uh-oh. That is bad news. Can you describe them
with a little more detail?"

"I knew enough to notice, and write it down immediately. They were both big, over six feet. One was real
wiry, thin but hard. Blue eyes, clean-shaven, but with a
heavy five-o'clock shadow. Big Jewish nose, pardon the
phraseology. Balding, jet-black hair. Scar on his neck,
like from a knife. Maybe 40 years old.

"His partner was chubby, not exactly fat, but with a
belly about to go over his belt. Sandy hair, full beard.
He wore shades, so I didn't see his eyes. He walked
with a slight limp on his left side. Maybe 30 years old.
Could be five years either way."

"Anything else? Accents? Peculiar speech or ges-
tures?"

Silence for a second. "Well, now, yes. The bearded
one didn't talk much, so I can't say. The wiry one came
from New England, most likely Boston. Had some trou-

ble with his Ls. Like Elmer Fudd, but not so much.''

"Anybody see this?''

"Well, you know. Thousands walked by, but saw nothing. The boys didn't make any overt moves.''

"Yeah, right. Do me a favor. Call the cops. Tell them everything, and tell them I'll call them. And, I'm really sorry. I wouldn't've had this happen to you for anything.''

"Lenny, me lad, I am taking an unscheduled vacation. I will call someone to take over the dog wagon, and I will be going to visit a friend. I won't say over the phone, but I think you know this person, and can get ahold of me if you need me.''

He was going to see his sister in New Jersey. This was the only place he ever went, if he was not at home.

"Take care. I'll say a prayer to Saint Paddy. And Seamus? Be careful. Take some evasive action when you travel. Switch buses, or cabs, or what-have-you, a couple of times. Crude, but effective.''

"This would definitely be more fun and excitin' if it were happening to you. Later.'' Click.

I thought things over for a few minutes. I called the local FBI office, and got the number of the Justice Department Office of Special Investigations. These guys track ex-Nazis for Uncle Sam.

A call to Washington elicited more than polite response only after I mentioned the name ''Dorfler.'' I was transferred to a Special Agent Clarke.

I introduced myself, and ran down what I knew. Clarke responded.

"Mr. Schneider, we've been bird-dogged by the Dorfler boys for years. At one point in time, we believed that there was a leak in this office. During some investigations, they showed up just before us, with negative consequences for the intended target. In these cases, 'target' took on a second level of meaning. We found one old guy in Ambler, Pennsylvania, with 37 9-mm. slugs in him.

''We were never able to prove conclusively that this old man was either a war criminal, or collaborator. Dorfler's people require far less evidence to, um, impose sentence.

''The good news is that we know the man with the Boston accent. If your friend'll file a complaint against him, we can get him off the street for a while, maybe sweat some info out of him. He's committed a crime by threatening, and we might be able to put something together based on the interstate nature of the user network threat. If this ties him to Dorfler, so much the better. Dorfler's never been touchable, so far.''

I was not able to get the name of the Bostonian. Agent Clarke was not forthcoming with anything else, either, so I got the name of his NYPD contact, thanked him, and signed off.

I had a head full of ideas that were driving me insane. I needed to think some more.

twenty-six

THE REST OF THE AFTER-
noon passed in business activities. Totally mundane, but
necessary, especially given my recent proclivities for
non-paying work. I set up several process services for
the next day, and a quick, painless bodyguard session: I
was escorting a dowager to a will-reading, about an
hour's work, for which I would receive $500. Genghis
Cohen might get her rent on time this month.

Having concluded the professional portion of my day,
I ventured to feed the inner man. The Old Kiev seemed
right. The Old Kiev is one of the mysteries of life in our
big city. It is a run-down looking restaurant on Avenue
A, opposite Tompkin's Square Park. I don't know how
long it has been there. It was old when I moved into the
neighborhood.

There is a counter, a row of booths, and a couple of
free-standing tables. The floor used to be linoleum,
somewhere around the Truman administration. Now, it
is a palimpsest of scuff marks and spilled food, worn
through to the floorboards in several spots. At the end
of the counter, near to the kitchen, a display case holds

those foods prepared for take-out: sausages, pastries, and the like.

When you peer into the open kitchen, you are treated to the sight of four Ukrainian grannies in white uniforms and hair nets stirring enormous pots, or frying up something in large batches. The smells are euphoric.

The only thing this place lacks is a beer license. I drink seltzer when I am there. I had studzienina, a kind of pork-in-aspic, served chilled. With it, I ate rye bread, red cabbage, and a bowl of hot Uki borscht.

I bantered good-naturedly with the Soviet-emigree waitress, her grin a glory of stainless-steel teeth. Once more, when I paid the check, I was amazed at the lack of tax on the bill. This was the only place in town that did not tax meals. Damned if I know why. Anyway, that always makes me increase my tips. The waiters and waitresses have provided exceptional service to me over the years. Heaven forfend that this place ever close.

Back to the pad for a hot bath, and to catch the end of the news on NPR. I read a bit of a Charlie Parker biography, caught between admiration and disgust. Such genius, such destructive egomania, such need for the approval of others, and contempt for himself for needing it.

I wondered why so many of my culture heroes were so flawed as human beings. I marveled at the price of creativity, or, more accurately, why some lives are so enhanced by genius, and others so damaged by it. Then I realized that milkmen, carpenters, proctologists, and college presidents often have the same kinds of problems, but so few are scrutinized like a Bird, or Sinatra, or Lenny Bruce.

Then I stopped thinking and crashed early.

twenty-seven

THE NEXT DAY WENT AS usual. I served summonses to husbands in arrears of child support payments, rebuffed one physical threat from some dork who wouldn't take the summons, and politely declined a blow job from an old queen who offered to take out his teeth to enhance the experience. I congratulated myself on being a man of principle, when I wasn't interested in the offer. One man's corruption is another's working within the system.

At two o'clock, I picked up the old woman at the Plaza Hotel, and took her to a Park Avenue law firm. I stood discreetly in the back of the room as I heard the legal jargon fly around the ceiling. Some parts of the drone stood out: $142,000,000, General Motors preferred stock, the scraping of a chair and muffled curses as a disowned nephew hit the road.

The client filled me in on the sordid family history as we drove back to the hotel. I contrasted this to the people I had served subpoenas and summonses to that morning. Maybe Hemingway was right. Maybe the rich just have more money.

I got home about 5:30, opened a Brooklyn Lager, and sat very still for a while. Then, I went to a phone booth and called Seamus, who seemed to be doing much better. I promised to keep him updated.

Realizing that I hadn't cooked a meal in a while, I bought some fresh fish, redskin potatoes, and a bunch of asparagus. I poached the fish, boiled the potatoes in their jackets, and steamed the asparagus. A dill-yogurt sauce lightly covered the veggies, and more lager washed it all down.

Then, I realized that I hadn't called Mickey. I might take care of that on the morrow. And so to bed, fortified by a healthy meal, and several beers. I fell asleep watching a bad cable movie.

twenty-eight

I TOLD YOU ABOUT THE two lesbian psychics in my office building. They are Sister Arletta, Tarot Reader, Diviner of the Eternal Mysteries, and Two-Way Street to the Spirit World. It says that on her door. And Madame Yvonne, Palm Reader, Gazer into the Future, and Peephole into the Void. That's what's emblazoned on her door.

Arletta's real name is Arlene Gluckstern; Yvonne's is Yetta Berkowitz. I know this because I witnessed a document for them once, and it had their names on it. Arletta will only answer to that name. If you call her "Arlene", she feigns deafness. Yvonne's attitude is, "I don't care if you call me *pisher*."

Arletta was born in Philadelphia; Yvonne was born in Minsk. They met at a Yiddish sleepaway camp in the Catskills. Arletta was there because her rich Socialist parents decided that she needed to mingle with the working class; Yvonne was there because she threatened to beat the shit out of the social worker at the settlement house if she wasn't given one of the charity slots at the camp.

They were both 13 years old, born on the same day within ten minutes of each other. They fell in love virtually on sight, and never looked back.

Yvonne moved to Philly, much to the relief of her entire neighborhood, was sort of adopted by Arletta's parents, and attended the best schools wearing the best clothes in company with Arletta. They slept in the same bed. The parents never suspected a thing.

They marched to save Sacco and Vanzetti, to protest the trial of the Scottsboro boys, and sat at the feet of Eugene Debs, Norman Thomas, Clarence Darrow, Paul Robeson, Pete Seeger, and the rest of the gods of the leftwing pantheon that graced the Berkowitz residence.

They moved to Greenwich Village when it was still really something. Poets, writers, folksingers, and other loonies swarmed through their apartment. Alice Toklas made them brownies, while Gertrude Stein drank their wine and execrated their interior decorating scheme, described by Arletta as "Early Jewish Reign of Terror." To this day, Yvonne refers to Stein only as "That Fat Bitch."

They claim that Aldous Huxley gave them some mescaline in the 40s, which Arletta hated, and Yvonne loved. When Huxley told them that this was a quick way into enlightenment, Arletta replied, "So, who's in a hurry?" From that time, they have been deep into the occult, yoga, spiritualism, herbalism, vegetarianism, etc. Yvonne also has a yen for psychedelics, which she somewhat overindulged in the 60s. She blames "that Tim Leary asshole, who would've been a drunk if he hadn't found acid."

It was the arguments over spiritual discovery versus chemical shortcuts that precipitated their continuing dif-

ference over What is Out There, and the best way to dig
it. Arletta's worst experience was her Aleister Crowley
phase; Yvonne's was her flirtation with Dimethyltrip-
tamine.

So, they were now two old ladies who had lived more
and done more than the entire population of your aver-
age suburban town. Well, one old lady and Yvonne.
They both pop in from time to time, alone or together,
to shoot the breeze, or try some new potion on me, or
to complain about each other.

They are always entertaining, although their potions
usually taste like boiled leaves someone has plucked in
the woods. It was no surprise to me that this is exactly
what they were.

I almost got off on the wrong foot with Arletta. The
day I moved into my office, she and Yvonne were scop-
ing me out, and generally kibitzing. Arletta offered to
help me.

"If you need anything, just call me," she said, somewhat coyly.

Getting into what I thought was the spirit, I said,
"Come to my office after the movers leave, and be na-
ked."

She blushed, and said, "Oh, no, no! I'm a lesbian."

"Oh, really?" I asked. "From Beirut?" It slipped out
before I could control it.

Arletta looked horrified; Yvonne cracked up, thank
heaven. Since then, the little dears have been a part of
my life. Naturally, Arletta has been trying to effect a
reconciliation between Sue and me; Yvonne refers to
Sue as "That Little Snip."

When I ambled into the office the next morning,
Yvonne stuck her head in my door and said, "Hey,

Lenny. Some dipshit was here looking for you. After he almost broke the glass knocking on your door, he actually tried to break in with a Visa Gold Card. I told him your door only took American Express.''

I chuckled appreciatively. ''What did he look like, Yvonne?''

''Like my cousin Moishe.''

''Can you be a bit more specific?''

''You can be such a bourgeois asshole. Tall, dark, not handsome. Big schnozz. Receding hair. Strong hands, with big veins standing out. I offered to read his palm.''

Mr. Boston, I should guess. ''Oh, yeah? What'd he say?''

''Well, nothing for a second, so I reached for his hand. He snatched it back pretty quick, but you know what? He had no fingerprints. Really. It must be, like, skin grafts or something. Smooth as a shaved snatch.''

''You have a gift for metaphor. Anything else?''

''Nah, not really. He said he'd be back, and he split. Nice friends you got, no fingerprints.''

''Believe me, sweet cheeks, he's no friend of mine. He didn't say anything else?''

''Nah, or I woulda said. Wanna try something?''

''Oh, shit. What is it, boiled jock itch?''

''Would I give you something bad?''

''Goddamn right you would. I still can't get the taste of that last one out of my mouth.''

''Schneider, you need to eat more pussy.''

With that, she returned to her lair. Now I really had a lot to think about.

twenty-nine

THERE'S A CORK BOARD in my office that I use when I have a complicated case. I write elements of the case, people involved, dates, seemingly unrelated incidents, and I shuffle them around until it begins to make sense. It doesn't always work. There are times that you don't have all of the ingredients, or at least not a key one. Other times, the bad guy, or person, is a nutburger, and follows no discernible pattern. But, in general, it gives me a chance to assemble all of the details in one place, and prevents my forgetting a thing here or there. It's useful.

I did not invent this system. I stole it from a book, or movie, or something.

Anyway, it occurred to me that I hadn't even begun to do this for the Uncle Sol matter, the pit bull thing, or the Nicky Carmine affair. One more item and I would have been forced to use ''caper.''

So, I thought about it. In the back of my mind was an unformed plan to go down to the newspaper morgue and accumulate all the materials on pit bull attacks. I was certain that a large number of incidents where the dog turned on the owner would turn out to be Ferdie Rodriguez's doing.

Williams at K-9 Protex said he was "unhappy" with Rodriguez's dogs. I was guessing that poor Alice Costello was the only death from these pit bulls at Protex. I was also guessing that one would be all it would take to make Williams unhappy.

A quick look at the Yellow Pages confirmed that there were many, a page or more, guard dog firms in New York, no doubt with plenty more in the burbs. If Ferdie were able to place dogs at every firm, one killing/robbery per firm might seem like a terrible thing, but not necessarily a crime wave. Especially since pit bull attacks were becoming routine, were hardly ever reported anymore in the media, and the cops might not have any reason to make a connection beyond the bad dog syndrome. Besides, the guard dog agencies were not about to publicize something like this. Bad for business, eh what?

There was even the possibility that two attacks might occur in one firm before they decided to give Ferdie's pit bulls the heave-ho. People are such trusting souls.

I reached for the index cards, then came up with a better idea. I already had too much to think about, so, why not meet with Detective Jane Murphy, give her everything I knew, and indicate a strong hunch in the direction of Staten Island? I could get this case off my back—a freebie, to boot—and score some points with the new kid. The cop house on Ninth Street wasn't too far out of my way home, and was close to Dirty Ernie's.

I couldn't think of any negatives. Next case.

The Nicky Carmine thing was also a nonpayer, but it involved my life. I started scribbling. Not much. Nicky

and Kopetch. Old case, with junkie sister and accountant. Repeated concern with my Jewishness. Louie Carmine and a big question mark on the last card. Did he
have anything to do with this, or was Junior getting his
own merit badge on me? I fished around in my desk
drawer for a red felt-tip and underlined the question
mark. There.

After pinning the cards to the cork board, I began to
write down the Uncle Sol case items. Lots more here,
including the most recent stuff with Feeney, Yvonne,
and Mr. Boston. It occurred to me that this was another
fucking freebie, and also implied a threat to my safety.
However, I could no more let this one go than I could
let Mickey go. It seemed, somehow, a price to pay for
her.

Aw, shit. That wasn't right. I was doing this because
there was a real danger that the old man, and maybe
even his family, could be seriously hurt or killed. I wres-
tled with the notion that I should simply tell Goffin what
I knew, and have him ask for police protection. That
might be the best avenue after all. I couldn't insulate
him from Nazis, Dorfler's anti-Nazis, and Christ-knows-
what-all.

I called the Goffin residence. The phone rang about
eight times, and I was just about to hang up, when Goffin picked up the phone.

"Yes?"

"Uh, Mr. Goffin? This is Lenny Schneider."

"Lenny, boychik! Thank God. Look, you gotta come
over here. The cops are here. We got a phone tap on.
Uncle Sol is missing."

thirty

THE RIFF WAS THAT SOL
had been missing since Sunday night. The cops set up
a tap, and told the Goffins to say nothing to anyone.
Since I hadn't spoken to Mickey since the weekend, all
of this was news to me.

I told Goffin that I had some small things to attend
to, and would be there by evening. I called the answering
service and alerted them to pick up my phone.

I bopped down to the police station, and asked to see
Jane Murphy. Expecting a classic Irish cop, I was surprised to see a black woman about 35, maybe 40. She
was dressed in the female equivalent of the rumpled
brown suit. There was even a shine on the seat of the
skirt.

She took me back to her desk. The office held four
desks. As the new kid, she had the worst one: farthest
from the door, the coffee, the toilet, and the overhead
light. If there had been a window in the room, she
wouldn't have been near it, either. I sat in her extra
chair, which squeaked piteously when my butt hit it, and
every time I moved thereafter. It was barely less annoy-

ing than fingernails on a blackboard, but much louder.

"Are you the guy that gave us the dog tip?"

"Yes, ma'am."

"What's your interest in this, in the first place?"

I briefly described the beating, Alice's help, and the scene at her building when the dog killed her. I told her about Herman and Annemarie. She nodded in the right places, and didn't go "uh-huh, uh-huh" every few seconds while I talked. I hate that.

She offered me a smoke. I declined. She lit up a Marlboro with a cheap butane lighter and exhaled. Her eyes were on me all the time.

"So," she asked, "why are you here now?"

"Well, basically, I'm here to add a few things to what I told you. Have you got anything new since the time I talked to Costa?"

She made a face, and shook her head. "I just transferred down here from the Bronx. I gotta wet-nurse my replacement up there. He calls me all the time, whining about whatever. I finally told him today to take a long walk off a short pier. I got my own problems.

"I hated to leave a couple of those cases in the middle, but, hey, that's life. So, I'm here. Now I can concentrate on my own shit."

I put on my sincere face. "Look, nobody knows better than me how much work you guys have to do. I sympathize. I also know when you can do these things better than me. Robbery and murder are police matters, and I'm a peeper."

It was starting to pile up on the floor around us.

"Besides, it's really not my case. No one has retained me, and no one is paying me. So, I'm history."

She dumped her cigarette into a paper coffee cup. It hissed, and turned the coffee green.

"Whaddaya mean, 'murder'?" she asked. "This is a dog attack, right?"

She riffled through the case folder quickly, trying to extract morsels of information. Her eyebrows shot up.

"Ah-hah! This robbery thing is new to me. What's missing, emeralds? Can anybody identify them?"

I told her that the daughter bought the stuff for her mother and probably had bills of sale. She nodded, and made a note in a spiral notebook. Getting back on track, I ran down my idea about Rodriguez, his dogs, and a new speculation I added on the spot.

"It's just occurred to me that Williams said that Rodriguez went to each new site personally to train the customer. It'd be easy to take advantage of a customer's trust to get them to tell him what it was they needed the dog for. If it was valuables, jewelry, whatever, he might ask to see them, or where they were hidden, so he could evaluate whether it was worth ripping them off. You know, under the guise of professional advice he could sniff out potential victims."

Murphy's face showed nothing, but her body language said—tell me more.

"So, he knows where the goodies are hid, if they are worth ripping off, and what else is there? He comes back some time later, maybe makes an appointment, you know, like a follow-up on the dog? When he gets there, he sicks the beast on the customer, grabs the loot, and splits. If he's really smart, he might even have the victim get the goods out before the attack. Less time needed for the getaway.

"I'm making this up as I go along, but, do you follow?"

She shifted in her seat and sat on one leg like a teenager. She was scrawling like mad, but suddenly stopped.

"Wait a minute," she drawled. "Do you have any proof of all this? What are you basing this on?"

"Look, you're a cop. You do this for any length of time and you develop a hunch instinct. Mine has been working overtime on this. If I decided to keep the case, I would go to the newspapers and look up all the pit bull attacks and see if I could connect them with guard dog agencies. Then, I would try to connect the agencies with Rodriguez, which shouldn't be hard because I was told that he was the only supplier of the beasts in the area. If you can develop a list of stolen valuables from the victims' families, that should be enough for a warrant."

She got testy. "Yeah, yeah. You don't have to tell me how to do my job."

I composed my face to project a complete lack of irony.

"Sure, detective. Just jiving, you know?"

"Don't get me wrong. I'm a believer in citizen involvement, and all that crap. And, I do appreciate what you've done here. We'll take this and run with it."

"Okay," I said, "can you keep me posted?"

She gave me her card, and told me to call in a few days. I shook her hand, and I was gone.

thirty-one

I RAN BACK TO THE OF-
fice to check my messages before heading out to Brooklyn. The service told me that Sue called. I called her
studio.

"Yeah, hello?"

"Sue? This is Lenny."

"Oh, yeah, wait a sec. I've gotta put this stuff down.
I'm holding the phone with my shoulder."

A moment later, "Hi, I just called. . . ."

"Wait a minute," I interjected, "I don't have a lot of
time and there's a lot to tell you." I filled her in on the
threats to Seamus Feeney, the visit to my office by Mr.
Boston, and the disappearance of Uncle Sol. She reacted
strongly to the Feeney part, gasped when she heard
about the office call, and exploded when she heard about
Sol.

"Jesus fuckin' Christ, Lenny! What do you think happened to the old man?"

"Sue, I'm sure I haven't a clue. I'm on my way out
to Brooklyn the second I hang up with you. Do me a
favor and call Bruno. If it's at all possible, I want him

on call for the next few hours, at least. I may need the guy, but I hope not. The cops have a tap on the Goffin line, and they may be treating it as a standard kidnapping. I'm not quite sure how come they reacted so quick. Any ideas?''

"This is all too much. I mean, I haven't had a second to think about it, but, I don't know. . . .''

"Sue, if you've got one of your brainstorms, cough up. I won't yell at you if you're wrong.''

"Okay. How did this Boston guy know about you? I mean, he was hooked to Seamus by the computer link, but, like, is there any way that Seamus would've told them about you?''

"Not a chance. If he had, he would've told me about it. This's been bothering me, too. I can't come up with any rational explanation of how I'm identified.''

Sue gasped. "Oh, shit, I just thought of something. What if they've got Uncle Sol? He's been gone for a couple of days, right? They could get a lot out of an old man in a couple of days, and the Boston guy came to see you since he disappeared.''

"Hmmm,'' I hmmmed. "Well, the obvious question here is: How the fuck do they know about Uncle Sol? I hate this job, sometimes. My brain hurts. I gotta go.''

"Listen, watch your ass. They could be staking you out. They could definitely be staking out the Goffin place. Okay, look, I'll get ahold of Bruno. He called me last week and left a number that can reach him when he, uh, drops out of sight.''

"Thanks. Oh, by the way, how was the weekend?''

"It sucked. That fuckin' macho pig should have his dick chainsawed off, and I'm the gal what can do it. Some fuckin' revolutionary. The only thing revolting about him is his personality. And, if I ever hear Ruben Blades again, I blow lunch. I'll give you the gory details later. Get your ass out to Brooklyn, and, listen, don't get hurt or nothin'. I'm worried about you.''

I gave her the Goffin phone number and told her to call only if absolutely necessary. I arranged to call her later in the day. After activating the answering service, I grabbed a cab on 14th Street and headed to the Goffin place.

thirty-two

THE CABBIE DROPPED me right in front of the building. As I paid him, I took a quick survey of the terrain. Nothing at first viewing. When he pulled away, I dropped all pretense of casualness and took a good look.

I saw the late-model Plymouth sedan parked across the street and down a few cars, and I caught a glimpse of a walkie-talkie coming up to meet a shadowy face. The styrofoam coffee cups and Dunkin' Donuts wrappers strewn on the dashboard contributed nothing to their camouflage. I scanned some more, less secure about the other eyes which might be on me. They would be better hidden, and I saw nothing I could ID.

While I waited for the banshee-screaming elevator, I contemplated the guy sitting on the lobby sofa, pretending to read a paper in light that would foil an owl. Now I know what happened to the Dallas cops that guarded Lee Harvey Oswald. The elevator arrived, and I whispered, "The 'single bullet theory' sucks," as I punched my floor.

When the machine screeched to a halt on four, the

opening door divulged two large uniformed cops with riot guns. So much for any vestige of subtlety.

"You Schneider?" the bigger asked.

"Yup."

"This way," said the smaller.

He escorted me to 4C, and I swear, knocked the same secret knock we used as kids to keep girls out of our keen clubhouse. A plainclothes type grabbed my arm and ushered me urgently in. He closed the door behind me, and patted me down. Scowling, he led me down the hallway past the kitchen, through the dining room and into the living room, which was lit up like Yankee Stadium, and had only slightly more electronic equipment in it than Cape Canaveral.

Three obvious cop types monitored the equipment, which was all arrayed around the phone. Besides them, there was Goffin, Mickey, and, glory to the lord, Sister Mary Louise. Some official-looking guy stood off to one side and took me in. Looked like the Feds, maybe.

Mickey ran up to me and threw her arms around me. Goffin and the Sister exchanged a raised eyebrow. The G-Man gazed blankly.

"How's everyone doing?" I whispered in Mickey's ear.

"Not bad," she whispered back. "Thank God the Sister is here." Then she subtly licked my earlobe.

"Watch it," I breathed, "this is a socially awkward situation for a hard-on."

She separated from me with a truly raunchy look, and took me by the hand over to her father and Sister Mary.

I shook Goffin's hand, squeezing his arm with my other hand to lend comfort. Then I turned to the nun.

"Sister Sheena," I chirped, "Our Lady of the Jungle."

She gave me a hug and said, "Lenny, when Lou told me that he told you, I knew I'd never hear the end of it. How are you?"

We traded pleasantries. She was with a teaching order that wore a kind of updated, street-clothes habit. The thick stockings and sensible shoes did not disguise her slender, well-turned ankles. A kind of cap, not unlike a nurse's cap, sat on the back of her head, with a short veil of dark material trailing to her shoulders. Her auburn hair was cut into bangs, and tinged with grey. Her green eyes and fair, pure complexion were like emeralds floating in cream. I sure hoped her husband was nice to her.

Looking from one face to another, with a quick nod to Eliot Ness, I asked, "Who's gonna fill me in on this?"

Everybody started to talk at once, and the Fed held up a hand to quiet the room. "Well, Schneider, I am Special Agent Clarke. We spoke on the phone." He extended his hand to be shook. I complied, and he went on. "I have misgivings about having you here. I told Mr. Goffin that he should tell no one, but he blurted it out when you called." He threw a look at Goffin, who looked ashamed for him. Mickey and the Sister each patted a Goffin shoulder.

"Where's Uncle Sol?"

"We're assuming that the men who threatened your friend are holding him. We have good reasons for this belief. The dark, slender one with the Boston accent is Lester Farkas. He's the son of camp survivors, now dead. He has dual Israeli-American citizenship, and he fought in the Yom Kippur war. A volunteer. After the war, he stayed in Israel and became a riot-control officer policing the Arab prisoners. He found one with a copy of *Mein Kampf* in Arabic, and tortured him to discover what he knew about Nazis among the Arabs, and anywhere else.

"The trail led him to several other prisoners, and, finally, to a Syrian army major. At that point in time, Farkas extracted quite a lot of information using questionable methods, even for the Israelis. When his superiors found out, they quietly asked him to resign his commission. After all, this was what you might call extra-curricular activity. The Nazi data was not on the official wish-list, nor was he authorized to use such extreme methods."

"How extreme were these methods?" I interjected.

"The Israeli government is reluctant to supply details, but our sources indicate, among other things, flaying of flesh and sexual mutilation. Sorry, ladies."

Mickey paled, the sister shivered and rubbed her arms, and Goffin uttered, *"Oy, Gott!"*

"Well," Clarke continued, "the prisoner didn't survive the day after the torture stopped. The Israeli government briefly considered prosecuting Farkas, but decided that the effect of the story on the Arab governments and American public opinion wouldn't be worth any gains made from the trial. So, he was asked to leave."

"How does he fall in with Dorfler?" I asked, with some impatience.

Clarke looked miffed. Apparently, his idea of information transfer and mine were noncontiguous.

"I'm getting to that. When he arrived back here, he

hooked up with the Jewish Defense League, even though he considered them crude amateurs, just to get into the peripheral groups. The JDL has unofficial interface with more-extreme groups, and many of their members are involved with several of them.''

''I haven't heard much about JDL in a long time. I assumed they were a dead issue.''

Clarke stiffened. ''Well, Schneider, that's why the FBI continues to perform valuable service to America, despite the carping of the critics. We never let go.''

''Yeah, I'm sure you have someone stationed at the Rosenbergs' graves to make sure they don't sell more atom secrets to the reds.''

I held up my hand in response to Clarke's malevolent gaze. ''Okay, okay. I take it back.'' I crossed my fingers behind my back. The Sister caught it, and snickered. ''So, Farkas meets Dorfler through some JDL connection, right?''

Clarke nodded, scowling, only slightly mollified. He picked up the dropped stitch of his narrative.

''As I was saying, Farkas met Dorfler through a JDL connection. He moved his base of operations to Chicago and became—what—the chief of operations for the network. It suited both Dorfler and him just fine. Dorfler wasn't connected directly to any of Farkas's activities, and Farkas got the best info he could hope to have gotten anywhere. Several suspected ex-Nazis have met untimely ends, and we are trying to connect Farkas to all of them.

''So far,'' he sighed, ''without much luck. The man is smart and has no scruples.''

Yeah, I thought, things haven't been the same since J. Edgar died of homosexual panic. But I didn't say it.

I did say, "Who's the pudgy, bearded one?"

"That, Schneider, is Otto Dorfler, son of the Big Enchilada, but he's basically a lightweight. The way we hear it, Carl is hoping some of Farkas will rub off on the kid. Farkas tolerates him for the good of the partnership."

I ran all this through my brain. One question leapt out at me. Before I opened my mouth and let fly, I told Clarke that Farkas had visited my office, and provided the details. This brought occasional gasps from the Goffin/Mickey/nun trio. They had been following the whole thing, and gasping periodically, like a Greek chorus with emphysema.

Clarke wrote down some notes. As he did, I asked, "How the hell does this lead to Uncle Sol? He's got no connection to the Dorfler thing. Do you guys belong to a computer network?"

Mickey shook her head vigorously; Goffin shrugged and showed his palms.

"Well, Schneider," Clarke sneered ferally, "we have reason to believe that Mr. Vishniac contacted some of the same groups that we discussed before through a local chapter of JDL, whose members train in the same gym as him. And, if you ask me, you gave him the idea."

The Greek chorus sprung to my defense, but, truthfully, I believed: a) Uncle Sol was smart enough to do this on his own; and, b) Clarke might be right, anyway.

Clarke continued, "So, we think that they nabbed him to find out something about you, about Mr. Vishniac's information and plans, and to advance a possible agenda against Ernst Mueller. The visit to your office likely came after they, um, spoke to Mr. Vishniac."

"Look, do you have any idea where Farkas and the Dorfler kid are holed up?"

Clarke laughed a stage laugh, devoid of humor, but not of scorn. "Really, Schneider, you slay me! Assuming that we knew, do you think for a minute that we'd tell you? You've screwed this thing up enough as it is."

I shrugged. "Well, Agent Clarke, you got me there. I know the real pros are in charge, now. I remember a story my Uncle Herschel told me. He said that, back in the 40s and 50s, when he was still an active Communist Party member, 4 out of the 12 members of his cell were FBI. You know how he knew? They always paid their dues. Nobody else ever did. He told me that, without FBI money, the cell would have ceased to exist because there was no money for anything. Yup, thanks to Hoover, more protest signs, propaganda booklets, and mimeographed broadsides got done than would have otherwise been possible. Herschel believed that Hoover was more responsible for the continued functioning of local Communist cells in this country than Joe Stalin, 'cause others told him the same story. Too bad McCarthy never heard that."

I turned to Goffin and company. "I gotta go. I'll try to find Uncle Sol while the Red Menace here answers your phones. If Bruno calls, tell him to call me at home."

I hit the street, and caught a cab back to Manhattan. The driver went on and on about how he hated to hit a goddamn dog with his cab. He said there was more goddamn paper work for a fuckin' dog than for a person. He'd rather hit a person, any time. I pondered asking him what he charged for FBI agents.

thirty-three

Bʏ ᴛʜᴇ ᴛɪᴍᴇ ɪ ɢᴏᴛ ʙᴀᴄᴋ to the apartment, I would gladly have fed the cabbie to the dogs. Where was Ferdie Rodriguez when I really needed him? As Samuel Johnson said about a similar bore, "His ideas were concatenated, without abruption."

What made it worse was that I needed to think, and my monosyllabic responses went unheeded as hints. So, when we stopped in front of my building, I was angry and distracted.

I paid him off, and sent him on his way to light up someone else's life. I entered the building and heard my phone ringing. It was probably Bruno, and I needed to discuss strategy. I stuck the apartment key in the lock and was suddenly treated to the spacey, slightly sickening odor of chloroform, administered from behind by person or persons unknown.

I struggled vainly against the effects of the anesthetic, and the powerful grip restraining my arms. The sound of my ringing telephone got farther away as I fell down the well into the darkness. I could hear Jim Morrison singing, ''Before I slip into unconsciousness, light another cigarette. . . .''

My last thought was, sheesh, I don't even smoke.

thirty-four

J UST CALL ME "ANGEL OF the morning." Amid residual nausea from the chloroform, my awakening occurred in a basement room. Pipes ran along the ceiling, and the windows were high and narrow. I was handcuffed to one of the aforesaid pipes, and faced a window. It seemed to be dark outside. My blurry line of vision was entered by a large, bearded face.

"Hey," the face said, "he's comin' out of it."

"Stand aside," commanded another voice, and a vague shape answering the description of Mr. Farkas appeared in the middle distance. "Can you hear me, Schneider?"

I was as yet unable to answer. My tongue felt the size of a catcher's mitt, and my brain was performing a damage-control function. Farkas waited patiently for what must have been a week. Once more, he probed.

"Come on, Schneider. We didn't dope you that bad."

I formed a whole thought: I'm trying to clear my head. What came out of my mouth was more like, "Watrah keer hat."

Farkas waited a bit more. I tried again.

"Fahkiss. Jussa mint. Okay?"

"Okay. Meanwhile, I can brief you. You understand?"

I nodded my head, which sent a wave of nausea through me. But, I could understand him well enough to listen.

"We're in the home of a supporter. You've been here about two hours. Mr. Vishniac is upstairs, and he's quite comfortable. We'll hold on to him as long as necessary to compel your cooperation. We want Mueller, and we think you can lead us to him.

"You already know that we had some advance word that he was in New York, even before the old man spotted him. We don't know why he's here, what for, or even if he's still here, really. He could've gone already. So be it. That means we need to find out why he came. *Fahrshtayst*?"

I nodded my comprehension.

"Can you talk yet?"

I tried. "Uh, yeah, maybe yeah. I don't know what you want. Seriously. Got no clue. I was workin' on it, but didn't get much."

"Well, we'll be happy to take whatever you have, and use you to get more."

"What's that mean?"

"We're gonna use you for bait, Schneider. We got sources who tell us that Mueller might be holed up somewhere in the Bronx. You're gonna track down the lead, and we're gonna be right behind you. Just in case the Nazis know us, right? You're just a cheap rent-a-cop out of his league, so their guard will be down."

"What if I don't?"

"Mr. Vishniac will remain our guest. His treatment depends on you."

"Farkas?"

"Yeah?"

"What the fuck is the difference between you and the Nazis? You'll both torture and kill Jews to suit your purpose. The end always justifies the means to you guys. Get fucked, hard-on!"

The image I took to be Mr. Dorfler's little boy entered into my field of vision again, and he punched me hard in the guts. I threw up in his face, and then he really beat hell out of me, but didn't leave a mark. They needed me to be presentable, such as I ever am. So, I got the pre-Miranda NYPD treatment—a phone book on top of the head, whacked by a hammer; a broomstick wrapped in a towel, in the ribs; a final kick in the groin, accompanied by a laugh. Not mine.

I felt myself losing consciousness again, from a combination of pain and nausea. No Doors music this time.

thirty-five

AFTER MY SECOND NAP of the evening, I woke up feeling great pain, but at least the chloroform was gone, and with it the nausea. I was laid out on the basement floor: Every move I made opened up a new vein of pain. I gotta get out of this business, I thought. Maybe get a job as a tackling dummy for the Jets so I don't have to take so much punishment. At least my sense of humor was still functioning, albeit on a low level.

The windows indicated that the first grey light of dawn was in the sky. I heard something, and looked up to see Farkas coming down the stairs carrying, for Pete's sake, a toasted bagel with cream cheese and a cup of coffee. If you're gonna get captured, get captured by Jews; the food's better.

I groaned, by way of greeting.

"Well," Farkas chirped, "how's our little sleepyhead? Ready to play ball? Or, should I have the big, bad man spank?"

He knelt next to me, and the aroma of the bagel and coffee did not make me sick. In fact, I was hungry as a wolf. I wished I had lox for the bagel. And Bruno. And an assault rifle.

Lurching up to a sitting position, amidst agony, etc., I took the coffee and tentatively sipped it. That was fine. I reached for the bagel. My mouth said, "Howdy!" Farkas waited while I made short work of the bagel, and sipped more coffee.

"Okay, Schneider," he began, "this is how it's going down. I'm gonna let Otto accompany you to your apartment. You are gonna get your act together. Then, you and him are going up to the Bronx. The location is a typical bombed-out Bronx building, but there's supposed to be a Nazi group holed up there pretty comfortably, using the ruins as camouflage. The rest of the operation will be explained by Otto once you get there.

"You will definitely not fuck this up. I expect a call from Otto no later than five o'clock tonight. If this call does not come, the old man will be found in the East River with a note in his pocket blaming you for driving him to suicide. He's already written it, with some persuasion required."

"I hate to eat a man's food and call him scum, but, you are scum, Farkas."

Farkas grinned. "Sure, Schneider. I'm scum. I'm just what's needed to fight scum. You assimilated Yids are so complacent. You never had to listen to your mother shrieking at night from death-camp nightmares. You never had to put your father to bed when he got too drunk to do it himself, and all the time he's jabbering away in Yiddish about watching his family die and being burnt. At least scum floats on top, Schneider. It doesn't sink, like shit."

"Look, Farkas, if I were in better shape I could match

your witticisms, and try to counter your arguments. You think that I don't agree with your aims. But, I do. It's your methods I find questionable. There are legal ways to deal with these monsters.''

''Yeah, right. You'll be yelling for an attorney while they shove you into the gas chambers. I'm tired of this shit. Get your ass off the floor. Otto wants to take you for a drive.''

He yanked me to my feet, and pushed me in the direction of the stairs. My body responded adequately, and we were out a side door. I never got a chance to see into the house.

The driveway was right there, and Otto sat behind the wheel of a rented Chevy. I was instructed to lie on the back seat, face down. Farkas whispered some last-minute instructions to the goon, and we were off.

At least Otto was not as loquacious as that cab driver. After some time, and after crossing at least one bridge, we pulled up in front of my building.

thirty-six

Otto MADE SOME QUICK checks of my bathroom, and ensconced himself on my bed. He flipped on the cable and watched "Old Yeller." I bet he cries when the dog dies.

I moved through a shower and beard trim on autopilot. I was real preoccupied. I took a couple of pain pills, and stuck a couple more in my pocket.

I put on clean khakis and heavy shoes with steel toes. Whatever I could use to create an advantage in a fight, and not be too obvious, I wore. My belt had a heavy buckle, and I took my big key ring. The jacket I slipped on already had a taped roll of coins in the pocket, but Otto patted me down and relieved me of it.

"Okay, asshole, let's go to the Bronx. We got stuff to do." Otto moved me toward the door.

When we got out on the sidewalk, I looked around for any possible means of escape. The car was parked by a hydrant a few feet away, and time was short. It was still early enough that people were going to work, and I considered shouting like hell and running.

I shouldn't have wasted my time. As we got to the
car, someone threw something over my head, and hit me
with what felt like a blackjack. I went under, yet again.

You ever have one of those days?

thirty-seven

M Y FIRST THOUGHT AS I struggled back to consciousness was: This is getting monotonous. Now my head hurt again. I was also uncomfortable.

My hands were tied behind my back, tightly enough to make them numb. I had some kind of bag over my head, and it was hard to breathe, besides being hot inside there. I was also wedged between what was probably the back of a car seat and what was probably Otto. Probably Otto groaned and stirred. After a few seconds, Probably Otto cursed just loud enough for me to determine that he was no more creative or interesting than most people.

I leaned over to what I hoped was his head, and whispered, "Cool it, Otto. Let's see if we can figure out what's. . . ."

I never finished the sentence. A voice I didn't recognize barked, "Shut the fuck up!" and I got whacked in the shoulder with a hard, heavy object. Shit. This really was getting to be a drag.

The rest of the trip passed in relative silence, except for the road noises that arose from below the floor of the vehicle. Finally, we came to a halt, after an exceedingly bumpy stretch. I heard the rolling sound of a van door opening and I was pulled bodily from the thing and dumped on the ground. I heard Probably Otto receive the same.

Then, the unmistakable rasp of Nicky Carmine said, "Stand up, you Jew fuck."

Now, for the first time, I was really scared, I expected my whole stupid life to pass before me, but it didn't. A well-placed kick ended my reveries, and I struggled to my feet, not easy with my hands tied. My hood was ripped off, and I breathed free again.

Short-time comfort, at that. Nicky kicked me in the crotch, and I hit the ground. I felt like my family jewels had been in a soccer game. Vasectomy by Florsheim.

When I recovered sufficiently, Nicky ordered me to stand again. I was faster off the mat, this time.

"Schneider, old pal, you're in such deep shit that you couldn't believe it in a million years. You're gonna wish that your fuckin' old man never met your whore mother."

As Nicky bloviated obscenely, I subtly tried to look around. We were in what must once have been a warehouse. It was vast, and had windows well above floor level. The floor was stained concrete. A motley of thugs stood in loose formation, about five yards behind Nicky. An old man I didn't know stood at his elbow.

The gang, an assortment of butt-uglies, had a high percentage of shave-skulled bad-asses with uniformly mean faces. Lots of tattoos of iron crosses and swastikas. Oh, brother.

The old man, whom I took to be daddy, was terrifying. His face was a road map of hell, twisted into a permanent sneer. If the eyes are the windows to the soul, this guy's should be boarded shut.

He was lean, stringy. He wore old, dusty corduroy pants too long for him, so the backs of the cuffs were worn out from being walked on. His shirt was a nondescript cheap sport shirt buttoned at the neck, but with the sleeves rolled up to his elbows. As he stood taking in the scene, his hands clenched and unclenched. Occasionally, he would run his age-spotted hand through his thinning, unkempt, iron-grey hair. His stained dentures were snaggle-toothed. He squinted. This was definitely the old block off which Nicky was a chip.

Nicky continued to hold forth on my unhappy and short future until the old man laid a hand on his shoulder, then he stifled like someone had thrown his switch. The old man sidled up to me, and spoke in heavily-accented English.

"So, Schneider, we got you at last. Your luck's run out, and the games are gonna begin. My son's not very original, but he's thorough."

Nicky said, "Aw, Pop."

The back of my mind, still functioning in its Sherlock Holmes mode, registered that something was wrong here. Louie Carmine, presumably Italian, spoke with a most un-Italian dialect. In fact, Carmine sounded like an old Jewish man. Then, I noticed his forearm. Traced in a blurred blue was a concentration camp number, replete with crossed European 7.

In a stroke of revelation, I knew, frighteningly, that Louie Carmine was the old ass-kisser from the concentration camps—Lev Kaminsky, turncoat and stoker of human flesh.

If I didn't wet my pants at that moment, I probably

never will. I was beginning to experience real terror, and I didn't much care for it. I wondered if a hundred index cards on my cork board would have ever led me to this conclusion. I wondered if Sue could ever intuit this. I wondered how much time I had left to live, and, with a shudder, instantly had the answer: Not much, but too much.

Carmine/Kaminsky went on.

"We're gettin' a bargain here. We got you, and we got Dorfler's brat, too. We're gonna send pieces of him back to Chicago for a couple weeks, then maybe his head. His papa's been a pain in our ass too long now. Too bad you won't be here for most of this. I would keep you alive for a few days, but Nicky, he's got a hard-on for you and you prob'ly won't see the sun rise."

I opened my mouth to speak, and Nicky charged me, fist upraised. Daddy stopped him cold with a lifted finger.

"You got somethin' to say, say it."

I cleared my throat.

"I know I have the pleasure of meeting Louie Carmine. Do I also have the pleasure of meeting Lev Kaminsky?"

Kaminsky made an impressed face. "You ain't so dumb."

"Tell me something. Where's Mueller?"

Kaminsky laughed. "The rabbi'll be here soon. He wouldn't miss this. He don't get much chance to practice his trade, these days. And I don't mean readin' the Torah."

It dawned on me that Farkas was expecting a phone call, or Uncle Sol was going for a swim. Kaminsky was getting even more of a bargain than he knew.

"You wouldn't, by any chance, let me make a phone call, would you?" What's to lose? I figured.

"Schneider, Nicky told me what a smartmouth you are. I think it's time to let him at you. He's a good boy, and his birthday's comin' up."

Kaminsky stepped aside. Nicky elaborately pulled on a pair of leather gloves, and smacked me right in the nose. I felt a sickening crunch, and knew it was broken. Then, he made a gesture, and two large skinhead types came forward and took me by the underarms. They half-carried, half-dragged me to a distant corner, which was set up with various apparatuses whose function, I feared, was soon to become obvious.

As we reached the set-up, I heard a horrible scream, and I guessed that Carl Dorfler was about to get his first shipment. The skinheads looked back over their shoulders, and laughed. Really, you have to admire people who take such pleasure in their work.

I sniffed my painful nose tentatively, and inhaled the metallic aroma of blood. I looked down, and my shirt-front was red with the run-off from my ruined hooter. I got light-headed, and slumped in the grip of the two thugs. They yanked me up and untied my hands. They fixed my wrists to an unpleasant-looking tubular steel frame by attached cuffs, which suspended me above the ground so that I could avoid hanging only by standing on tip-toe. Nicky approached a table which stood along-side the set-up. The table was strewn with everything from medieval torture implements to cordless power tools.

After brief chin-scratching, Nicky picked up a cattle prod. Subtlety be damned. He walked over, and began one of his demented harangues, obscene, racist, simply deranged. In light of the imminent, I was content to listen attentively.

Suddenly, he lunged at my belly with the prod. A paroxysm of agony radiated from the point of contact. My hair stood up, and I thought my eyeballs would boil. Nicky shrieked like a kid with his first erection. The skinheads, who had been watching daddy work on Otto across the room, glanced back over their shoulders and nodded approval.

I believed it was going to be long day. He hadn't even begun.

Just then, the most amazing thing happened.

A tremendous crash resounded through the cavernous space as a vehicle blasted into the warehouse. Even Nicky was distracted. We all gaped at the sight of a large diesel truck with a steel plate reinforcing the front, and hauling a trailer, as it tore the corrugated metal door like cheesecloth.

It lurched to a halt in a squeal of airbrakes and tires, and men began exiting the trailer brandishing automatic weapons. Strike while the iron is hot, I thought, and I kicked Nicky in the belly, one more time. The skinheads didn't even look back. They drew guns and headed for the action.

A massacre ensued. I recognized Farkas among the confusion of shots and cries and chaos. In seconds, most of the Carmine gang was dead or incapacitated. A few of Farkas' commandoes were wounded, but their bulletproof vests had precluded fatal injury. These guys were pros. The floor was littered with writhing skinheads, or the corpses thereof. All were covered by Farkas' gunmen, jumpy and alert.

Now, I thought, get someone over here before Nicky

gets his wind back. Farkas himself ambled over. He took in the scene, and kicked Nicky in the face. Now Nicky's nose was smashed, and it made sickening bubble noises as he tried to suck in breath.

Without a word, Farkas got some bolt cutters off the supply table, and cut my wrists free. I slumped down, and lost consciousness.

thirty-eight

I DIDN'T KNOW HOW long I was out, but I awoke supine on the floor next to the huge truck. Farkas stood over me.

"You're a fucking mess. Can you get up?"

I tried, and slowly succeeded. I was a bit shaky on my pins, but the darkness at the edge of my vision was receding, and I wasn't dizzy.

"Jesus, Farkas. I'm think I'm glad to see you. What happened?"

"Well, we barely trusted Otto to babysit you, so we put a tail on the car. Just an observer, to make sure it all went down according to plan. We didn't know you were so in demand. Is there anybody in this town who isn't after you?

"Anyway, when these creeps nabbed you, they were obviously skinheads. We figured, what the fuck? We'll root out a nest of rats to make it a full day. Imagine our surprise and delight when they led us right to the main event. Can you tell me what's going on here?"

I related the chain of circumstance that had led to my involvement with Nicky, and that his family affiliations included more than I had anticipated. We both mused briefly on the power of coincidence.

A thought flashed. I exclaimed, "Oh, shit! Ernst Mueller is supposed to be on his way here. He was gonna work some SS magic on us."

Farkas was galvanized. He ran to a burly guy in a fatigue jacket and spoke excitedly. Orders got shouted here and there, and several commandoes ran out of the building.

Farkas came back over. He thought for a minute, and said, "Schneider, there's a good possibility that Mueller spotted the operation, and scrammed. My boys are out combing the area, but I doubt that they'll find anything. Shit. It really would've felt good to get him, too."

"Farkas, something's been on my mind, but I haven't given it much time because I had other things going. Mueller had a concentration camp tattoo. Or LeVine did. Assuming they are one and the same, how does he get a number on his arm?"

"Mueller was SS, right? Well, the SS got a tattoo also: the Lightning SS, on their forearms. After the war, this became a real problem. The SS were war criminals, and they had this distinguishing mark. So, bunches of them faked a camp number, using the jagged esses as fours. You know, just lengthen the line of the S on the right side, and it passes for a four, especially if you aren't looking for it. These fuckers were real clever then, and they still are.

"That's why we have to exist. The world made us, Schneider. Me, and all these other guys, also, would rather be home drinking a beer and watching the Red Sox, or the Mets, or whatever. But, because the CIA let in so many Nazi scum, and because Jews like you no longer give a shit, justice has been aborted. Never mind miscarried, aborted.''

He looked into my eyes, through the back of my head, maybe.

"Never again, Schneider. That's not some fuckin' slogan. Never. Fucking. Again.''

I changed the subject. "How's Otto?''

Farkas twisted his mouth into a smirk. "He'll be okay, unless he has plans to be toe dancer.''

In spite of myself, I snorted a laugh. If this guy wasn't such an unprincipled, cold-blooded menace, I could like him. I had another question.

"What are you gonna do with Kaminsky?''

"Oh, yeah. I almost forgot.''

He called out, "Herb! Bring Kaminsky over here, and our other guest over here.''

Kaminsky, his hands tied behind his back, was hauled out of the trailer and shoved over to a spot in front of the giant truck. Then, from around the back of the truck, the man called Herb escorted Uncle Sol. Sol's face, as usual, betrayed no emotion. That is, until he saw Kaminsky.

Blood rose in his face. He said, through clenched teeth, "Kaminsky! *Choleria! Momser! Meesa mash-inna!*''

The Yiddish abuse was doubly insulting to Kaminsky. He glowered. He had no idea who this was, but it was clear that his contempt didn't require personal knowledge.

"Jew bastard! You must be one I missed in the camp.''

Kaminsky turned to the man holding him. "Untie me.

I'll kill you one by one, startin' with this old piece a shit.''

The captor looked over, and Farkas nodded. Kaminsky's ropes were cut. He smiled obscenely, and rubbed his wrists.

"Farkas!" I yelled. "What are you, fuckin' nuts? Animal! How can you. . . ."

Farkas smacked me across the face.

"Shut up! They both want this. Butt out!"

"Uncle Sol!" I yelled. "Don't do this. Don't be like them."

"Mind your own business, Mr. Schneider. Lev and I will take care of our own."

The two old men faced each other; like scorpions in a bottle, neither one might emerge. The poison was too strong, the hate too abiding.

They began to circle, arms held like wrestlers, neither willing yet to make a first move. I sized them up. Sol was in good physical shape, and had recently been given some training in martial arts, but Kaminsky was psychotic, and knew no mercy. Each was driven by some atavistic loathing, not only for the other, but for what each represented. It was like a medieval *auto-da-fe*, two champions of conflicting philosophies squaring off to prove whose side God was on.

More to the point, it was two old men about to try and kill one another, being egged on by a crowd of amoral vigilantes. Pathetic, and damaging to the soul.

Kaminsky lunged, and Sol neatly sidestepped the charge, delivering a blow to the back of Kaminsky's neck. Kaminsky wheeled, his face contorted. It was the original version of Nicky's cornered-rat snarl. Also, the most terrifying look I ever saw on a human face. Sol crouched, ready.

Kaminsky hurled himself through the air. The force of his leap knocked Sol over, and the two sprawled on the concrete floor. The crowd of onlookers yelled like spectators at a prize fight.

The old men rolled and struggled, each looking for some advantage. Kaminsky, moving like a rattlesnake, bit off most of Sol's right ear and spat it on the ground. The crowd loved it.

Blood was everywhere as Sol finally exerted himself to pin Kaminsky to the ground. He struck Kaminsky's throat with a knuckled fist, and a sickening crunch announced that the larynx had been crushed. Kaminsky gasped horribly. He worked one arm free, and clawed Sol's cheek with his septic nails.

Calmly, like a diamond cutter, Sol gouged out both of Kaminsky's eyes with his thumbs. I turned my head and puked. Farkas snickered.

Finally, deliberately, in what appeared to be slow motion, Sol grabbed Kaminsky's hair and began to smash his head on the floor. As he did, he began to chant, rhythmically, from the Hebrew ceremony for the dead, the *Yiskor*. He punctuated the rhythm with head smashes. His face was in a transport, almost an ecstasy of grace, angelic and grotesquely shaded by the blood running from the ripped cheek and missing ear.

Sol was as crazy as Kaminsky. If he lived, I doubted he would be fit for human company ever again.

The crowd pulled Sol off of Kaminsky when it was clear that the man was dead. A spreading puddle of blood moved from under what was left of Kaminsky's head. Sol looked down. He uttered a great sob, and collapsed.

Farkas said, "Okay, boys. Show's over. Let's get out of here." He looked at me. "Schneider, I still haven't figured out what to do with you, so you're coming with us. Dave! Marty! Blindfold Schneider and take him back to HQ."

Two men dragged Nicky over to where his father lay on the floor. Nicky screamed and then began to cry. I almost felt sorry for him.

Farkas walked over. "See, Nicky Boy, Jews are pretty tough, after all. Good riddance to scum." Farkas grabbed Nicky's head, and expertly broke his neck with a quick motion. Nicky joined his father on the floor.

Farkas yelled, "Throw the old man in the car with Schneider. And, don't forget his ear."

Somebody blindfolded me. I was half-dragged outside the building, and thrown into the back seat of a car. I felt Sol's limp body slump against me.

I also smelled the rank odor of gasoline as they prepared to torch the place. In the South Bronx, no one will give a shit. I wondered if the cops or fire inspectors would even investigate the charred corpses.

Two guys got in the car, and we drove off.

thirty-nine

WE DROVE FOR A WHILE,
and then got onto a highway. I presumed, owing to the
deplorable condition of the road, that it was the Cross-
Bronx Expressway, but in what direction I could not
guess.

As we drove, I ran events over in my mind. I was one
hurtin' unit. My nose was broken, and who knew what
else. Uncle Sol had lost a lot of blood, and, more im-
portantly, his reason to live. Mueller was probably still
at large, but I was sure that Sol lacked the killer urge
any longer.

Mueller would go wherever Nazis go. Maybe South
America, but there were plenty of sympathetic gringos
north of the border who would be honored to shelter
him. Farkas and his merry men would go on wreaking
50-year-old revenge, unless Special Agent Clarke caught
up with him, an event I saw on the same level of prob-
ability that Elvis would run for Congress.

And what would become of me? I knew that Farkas'
respect for human life was nil. If Kaminsky had won
the fight, Farkas would simply have killed him on the

spot. All Uncle Sol did was provide some entertainment before the inevitable. So, my chances of actually having another meal at Chen's were not good. I was incredibly hungry, and the thought of Chen's food heightened the exquisiteness of my agony.

The car apparently pulled off the highway. We slowed down, and began to drive on streets. I hadn't a clue where we were. If it's time to buy it, who cares? It's all New Jersey.

Then, the formerly silent driver screamed, "Hey! What the fuck does that guy think he's doin'?"

I could feel the car swerve. "He's tryin' to force us off the road. Marty, shoot the bastard!"

Before Marty could shoot the bastard, the car lurched wildly, and skidded. The sounds of flying gravel striking the car preceded a scream from the front seat.

Then the car slammed into something, and I don't remember anything after that.

forty

 F OR A COUPLE OF DAYS I
drifted in and out of consciousness. An impression of a
hospital grew stronger as the moments of lucidity in-
creased in length and number. I have images of nurses,
fleeting pictures of Sue and Bruno and Goffin and
Mickey and Sister Mary Louise.

But, I also have memories of seeing my mother, who
is long dead, and Gil Hodges, ditto. Gil was my hero
and idol as a kid. He was the first baseman for the
Brooklyn Dodgers during their glory days. He eventually wound up managing the Washington Senators and
the Mets. If that didn't assure him a place in heaven,
nothing will.

During the 1952 World Series, poor Gil went oh-for-
twenty-two. And he was a good hitter. All over Brooklyn, there were prayer services for him so he would get
a hit. All to no avail. The friggin' Yanks won to boot.

The reason people prayed for Gil was that he was a
gentle and kind man besides being the best first-sacker
of his time. He was well-loved by the baseball world
and by his fans. Except for my mother, and maybe my

Uncle Murray, he was the biggest influence on my young life.

So, Gil entered my hallucinations during those strange hours. I guess I'll never be able to sort the visions out.

One clear thought dominated the experience—God-damn, I'm alive! It occurred to me at least once in every episode of wakefulness. It was a comfort amidst the confusion.

When I finally awoke for real, it was early the morning of the third day. I was immediately aware that I was restrained in my bed. Painfully, and with a wash of nausea, I lifted my head, and took stock of myself.

My right hand was lashed to the bedframe, and sported a cast from wrist to elbow. The left was similarly tied, but without a cast. My breathing was restrained by some kind of binding around my torso. My legs were under a sheet, but a gingerly test movement confirmed that they were tied down. My nose was bandaged, and maybe packed. I thought I felt bandages around my head.

There was not much pain, just an unfocused dull ache almost everywhere I concentrated on. With a sick feeling, I noticed that I was catheterized, and that there was a tube entering my arm from a suspended bottle. I couldn't read the label. I did remember The Soldier in White, from *Catch 22*. I wondered when they would come in to switch bottles.

The wait wasn't long. A youngish nurse entered the room. I planned to tell her that I was okay, but a harsh croak was all that escaped my throat.

''Well, Sleeping Beauty's back in the land of the living. You can't talk because you haven't had anything by mouth in days, and you're probably a bit dry. Do you want some water? Hot tea?''

''Wah.''

''Okay.'' She poured a glass from a plastic decanter, and put in one of those flexible straws. ''Sip this, but don't overdo it. Just a little at a time.''

She continued to coo at me while I let the cool water trickle down my throat. I could feel my arid mouth absorbing moisture. My stomach growled angrily when the water hit it.

''My, my,'' she said, ''Mr. Tummy is cross. I'm afraid you'll have to be fed intravenously until the doctor reevaluates you today.''

''Any way,'' I whispered, ''you can put a corned-beef sandwich and a knish in the bottle?''

''Everyone says that you're a wise guy. I guess they're right.''

''Where am I?''

''River View Medical Center. You were brought in by ambulance from the scene of a wreck. Mr. Vishniac is in the next bed.''

I whipped my head around to the left, fighting a wave of nausea, and there was a pale face surrounded by mummy wrappings in the next bed. I could see his chest move.

''How is he?''

''Very lucky, if you ask me. More than you. We're still trying to figure out how his ear was severed, but we think we were able to save it. His other injuries were pretty trivial, considering. After all, the two men in the front seat both had broken necks. What the hell happened out there?''

''You don't want to know, and I'm in no shape to tell

you right now, anyway. Can you untie me?''

"Oh, yeah, sure. We had to restrain you because of
the way you were thrashing around in your sleep. You
established a new indoor record for colorful vocabulary
in this hospital. You're worse than the women in natural
childbirth, and more creative.'' She busied herself with
the straps.

"Just my luck I wasn't able to appreciate it,'' I
rasped. ''Tell me, is Mr. Vishniac conscious?''

"Oh, yeah. He's asleep, but he's been improving
steadily. He's a tough old bird.''

"You don't know the half of it. Can I have some
tea?''

"Sure. I'll be right back.'' She reached behind my
head. ''Here's the call button. Can you move your fingers?''

I wiggled them satisfactorily, and she laid the button
in close reach. She looked down at me.

"Who's Bobby Thomson, and why should he go
straight to flaming hell?''

"Jeez, did I say that? Well, it's an old story. He's a
nice old man, and I've forgiven him. I can't believe I
said that.''

"Wait'll I tell you some of the other stuff. And wait'll
you get a load of what the night nurse heard.''

I smiled wanly. She left, and I looked over at Uncle
Sol. I tried to convince myself that he looked at peace.

Then, he stirred. I lifted my head to get a better angle.
He opened his eyes, saw me, and smiled. In a soft, dry
voice he said, ''It's good to have you back, Mr. Schneider.''

"Call me Lenny, Uncle Sol.''

"Lenny.'' He smiled again. I realized that it was the

first time I had actually seen him smile, and I wondered how long it had been since he felt like smiling.

As the hospital wheeled into its regular morning routine, Uncle Sol and I had a heart-to-heart. Barely interrupted by bustling staff, we discussed what happened. I sipped my tea.

"Lenny, what happened is a mystery to me. For years I was a bitter man. My family massacred. Nobody can go through the camps and be normal. After the war, I never recovered, or got on with my life. I lived in name only. A black cloud was inside my head. I'm embarrassed to say, but when I met other camp survivors who had more-or-less adjusted, I felt contempt, anger.

"Now, I'm sorry for the waste. I wasted a university education, I became a burden on my nephew, Louis. A shame."

"Don't be so hard on yourself. Everyone has to heal in his own time. Your time has come, that's all."

"No, no. You don't understand. All this is just since my fight with Kaminsky. It was like, I don't know, lancing a boil. All at once, came out the poison. The second after I, *oy Gott*!, broke his head open, I was so ashamed. The scales fell from my eyes. I wanted to die, myself. Forty years of venom and hatred I saw in one second."

"Uncle Sol, I have no experience to compare with yours, so it's just common sense. If you can, begin again. Don't undervalue your, ah, cure. If the poison is gone, be an uncle, be a whole person. Be a *mensch*. Lou and Melanie will help you."

"Maybe I'll be an artist. Already I got the ear missing."

I laughed out loud. I remembered Goffin telling me

what his mother said about Sol—the old Sol—always with the jokes.

"Uncle Sol, when you feel up to it, Melanie and I will take you to a ball game. Baseball is great way to forget your troubles. Compared to the Yankees, you're in great shape."

A white-clad employee wheeled in a tray with breakfast plates, each covered with a metal top. He served Sol. Cold cereal with whole milk, coffee, a toasted muffin.

"Hey," I asked, "you got a short stack with a side of sausage and an egg over easy?"

The server, a wiry Hispanic, myopically peered at his chart. "For you, my fren', I got lime jello." He pronounced it like "yellow."

"Sold." I reached out hungrily. Just then, Sue walked in.

"Lenny! You're awake. Are you all right?"

"Sue, baby, good to see you. Yeah, I'll live. Just don't enter me in the twist contest for a while."

Satisfied that I was alive, she immediately turned her attention to the other bed. "Solomon, sweetheart, how are you today?"

"Susseleh, come give me a kiss."

Susseleh? Kiss?

She went over to Sol's bed, gave him a big, wet smooch, and the two of them chattered away like old friends. Worse. Like old lovers. You know, lots of soft touching and sweet glances.

My ex-wife has the facility to endear herself to anyone in a moment. It takes a while to appreciate fully her capacity to make you want to kill her. Clearly, Sol was nowhere near that point.

After they caught up on all the goings-on since yesterday, Sue turned to me. "God, Lenny, how do you get into crap like this? If you hadn't gotten into this racket, we might have made it."

As usual, her memory was selective, but this was not the place to remind her of her lapses.

"Yeah, well, I got into this trying to keep your boyfriend over there from getting himself killed. Did I do a great job, or what?"

"Don't you blame this on Solomon. Let some other private eye do this. Stick with the easy stuff. Maybe you should start an agency, and hire people to risk their lives."

In my weakened condition, I was half-inclined to admit the intelligence of this suggestion. But, naah. I wasn't ready to become a middle-aged entrepreneur quite yet.

"Susseleh," Sol put in, "don't be so hard on Lenny. He's a brave young man, and wiser than you know."

"Yeah, lay off. At least until I get myself together, and get out of here. Can somebody explain what went on the last day I was semi-conscious?"

Sue sat on the edge of my bed. She reached into her bag and took out a little spiral notebook.

"What's that?" I asked.

"I keep notes on every case you talk to me about. This is, like, my fourth or fifth notebook. Okay, first the stuff from the answering service. An Annemarie Garfolo called. She said to tell you that Jane Murphy called her to say that they caught the guy who killed her mother. Lenny, how can you stand this business? Also, she said that she was gonna introduce Herman to her Aunt Connie at Enzo's wedding, and that you could come, too, if you wanna. Do you understand any of this? Anyway, she left her number. And she said 'Thank you very much'.''

She wet her thumb and turned the page.

"Next case. Jane Murphy called. She said to thank you for your citizen involvement, and that Rodriguez was sitting on a load of stuff he hadn't fenced yet, and that forensics was working on the dog attacks. She said it looked good, and that you should call her.''

Lick. Shuffle.

"Weezil Furnham sent a telegram. Is this that guy you used to talk about? Anyway, he's coming back to the States from Bingo Bongo, or somewhere, and he wants to start a dance troupe. Do you know anyone normal? And Seamus called, and I told him what was going on, and he decided to stay where he is a bit longer. He was real mysterious. Is Weezil the guy who lost the spelling bee?''

I nodded. She nodded. She went on.

"Last, and definitely least, Rifke Cohen came around to tell you that the rent is going up. That woman should have her wardrobe cleaned and burned. Homeless women dress better than her.''

"Okay, never mind the fashion commentary. What the hell happened the other day? I mean, do you actually know?''

She gave me a look like I had impugned her professional integrity.

"Well, I made a couple of educated guesses here, but this is probably close. You told me to call Bruno. I got him right away, and gave him the story. So, he told me that he was gonna call a friend of his to keep an eye on your place. Then, he was gonna call you to make plans.

So, when he called, there was no answer.''

''Yeah, the phone in my place was ringing when Farkas's people swiped me. That must've been him.''

''He. That must've been he.''

''He, shme,'' I said in an impatient tone. ''What's next?''

''Okay, so Bruno kept in touch with his guy by car phone. The guy tailed you to some place in Queens or Nassau County. You were in there for hours. I told Bruno that they might be holding Solomon, so not to do anything rash. Bruno said they were observing the house and would wait, and then play it by ear if something happened. Wait a minute.''

She consulted her notes.

''Okay. I got it. That's when Bruno called me. He told me to call Goffin's and alert the Feds, but not for a couple of hours. He told me he was curious about what they wanted from you. Besides, he thought they might go in like Gangbusters and screw things up. He said he would signal me when to call.''

She sure was cleaning up her language. Uncle Sol might be a good influence on her.

''Bruno followed the car you were in, and had an, um, associate stay with the house to keep an eye out for Solomon. He was quite amazed when you went back to your place, and even more amazed when the goons got you and the other guy. He recognized them as skinheads from Louie Carmine's gang. But, he was really flipped out when they took you up to The Bronx to the hideout. It was really a well-kept secret, the hideout. Nobody knew where it was. Well, maybe a general idea, but as to . . .''

''Will you get on with it?''

"Oh, yeah, sorry. So, anyway, Bruno observed the hideout from a rooftop across the street. He really couldn't see inside from where he was, so he was preparing to try to get inside when that humongous truck showed up. That blew his mind. In the confusion, he was able to slip inside and hide himself. How does someone that size hide?"

She reached over for a glass, and poured herself some water from the carafe. She sipped.

"Yich. Tastes like bathroom water. I wonder why bathroom water tastes different? You ever notice?"

"Suuuue, puh-leeze."

"Solomon, this is why our marriage broke up. This man has no patience. Well, now, where was I? Oh, okay. So, Bruno saw you and decided that you were a tough guy and would survive. Besides, he was outnumbered, big-time. He said he didn't even have an extra clip for his gun. When they took you and Solomon out he followed, but he made sure that his crony stayed with Farkas. This guy that came up to The Bronx following Farkas and Solomon. Bruno told the guy to call me and tell me where the truck was going, and to tell the Feds.

"So, they took you up to Westchester, maybe to some safe house, but Bruno ran your car off the road. He said he neutralized the two in the front. What did he mean by that, 'neutralized'?"

I spread my hands in an "I don't know" gesture. She could be spared some things.

She shrugged. "Well, Bruno called the nearest hospital, made sure you were safe in the emergency ward, and split before anyone could ask questions. He called Clarke. He called me and told me where you were. And, here we are."

"What happened to Farkas?"

"Oh, the FBI got him at some trucking terminal in Sunnyside. Him and all his boys. They're in deep shit. Excuse me, Solomon."

"Clarke got Farkas! Damn! If you see Elvis, tell him he's got my vote."

Sue squinted at me. "Huh?"

"Uh, never mind." I felt real calm, for the first time in a while.

Sue's narrative had worn me out. I squeezed her hand, and said, "Thanks, baby. That was a very thorough report. Do me a favor and let me get some rest. Uncle Sol probably needs it, too."

Sue stood up. "You got it. I have some work to do. My whole life has been on hold for the last few days. Goodbye, Solomon."

She kissed him, kissed me, and was out the door.

"Lenny, what a cutie. If I was 30 years younger . . ."

"I got news, Uncle Sol. She could age you back in two weeks. I'm glad to have her around, but I'm also glad we're not married any more. Has she met Melanie yet?"

"No, but I'm looking forward to that."

"You're an evil old man. Let's get some rest."

forty-one

THE NEXT DAY PASSED in relative ease. I was not well enough yet to be antsy and Uncle Sol kept me from being bored. His stories of life in pre-Nazi days were funny and bittersweet. The time drifted lazily.

Visitors came and went. Lou Goffin, Mickey, Sister Mary Louise, Sue, even Seamus and Bruno. The staff was nice and relatively unobtrusive.

The day nurse was delightful. The night nurse was a sardonic middle-aged black woman who insisted that I ranted obscenely for two nights while I was fighting back from Never-never Land. Her religious scruples prevented her from being more specific, except to say that I had carried on a sexual conquests conversation with an unseen Charlie Parker, and that she wished she could have heard his end of it.

The day after I came to, I was devouring solid food exclusively. "Solid food" is about all the credit I will give it. I was saved from death by culinary insult by the occasional Kosher hot dog or pastrami sandwich smuggled in by one or another visitor. I had to split some stuff with Uncle Sol until I got the message out to bring two of anything.

The day nurse generally turned a blind eye to these transgressions, except when Seamus smuggled in a quart of home-brewed stout. She drew the line at that.

The morning of the next day, the nurse came in more sprightly than usual.

"Well, Mr. Schneider, I am happy to tell you that, pending the results of some tests we will do later, you can probably leave tomorrow. Mr. Vishniac will likely be here a few days more, but he could be gone by the weekend.

"I'm sure you are both happy to hear that. I know that the staff will certainly welcome a return to something like normal routine in this wing. Every time that large man comes in here, the candystripers hide in the ladies' room."

"Bruno has that effect on people. That's one reason I find him so valuable. He's really quite gentle, as long as you're no threat to him. Of course, I never told him that you confiscated that beer. . . ."

She rolled her eyes in mock terror.

"God! I promise never to do that, again. Meanwhile, since we at the staff have real fears for the fate of your eternal soul, we arranged for our new rabbi to pay you a visit. He's usually here about one o'clock."

Uncle Sol raised up on one elbow. "You know, I might like that. I haven't had a civil word for a rabbi in forty years. Maybe it's time to bury the hatchet."

"He's all yours, Uncle Sol. As a practicing atheist, I am interested in the clergy only from an anthropological angle."

The nurse made a face. She wagged a warning finger

at me, and left. Sol and I dozed a bit until lunch, and polished off the mystery casserole with more hunger than relish.

We awaited the nourishing of our spirits.

forty-two

ABOUT ONE-FIFTEEN, THE nurse ushered in an elderly man, goateed, stooped, with horn-rimmed glasses. He was dressed in a three-piece banker's suit, a gold watch chain corralling a respectable paunch. He peered through his glasses, first at me, then at Sol.

"Thank you," he said to the nurse, in heavily accented English.

She nodded at the rabbi, and said, "Watch out for these two, rabbi. They might corrupt you. Especially this hoodlum," indicating me with a gesture.

The rabbi chuckled. "I have handled worse than this before."

The nurse left. The rabbi walked over to Sol's bed. Sol sat up, with some effort. He extended a hand to the rabbi.

"Solomon Vishniac, rabbi. A pleasure."

"Sit down, rabbi," I said. "Pull up a chair." Because I didn't 'believe' was no reason to be rude.

His eyes narrowed slightly, as he took me in. "Thank

you," he said. He dragged over a chair and placed it between the beds.

There was a moment or two of awkward silence. Then the rabbi began to speak.

"Mr. Vishniac, the staff tells me that you have been through a trying experience. They also said you were in the camps. I, too, was there."

Despite his load of bandages, Uncle Sol squirmed a bit. It seemed like he was still uncomfortable discussing his life with a stranger.

"I'm sorry," he managed.

"Of course," replied the rabbi. "The experience affected my whole existence since then. I don't have to tell you. Since then, I have dedicated my life to helping victims."

Slowly, a conversation between the two men developed. I was not directly involved and I started to tune out and drift off to sleep. I caught only snatches.

One snatch pulled me back from dreamland. Uncle Sol asked, "So, rabbi, where is your congregation?"

The rabbi hesitated. "I, uh, presently don't have one. I volunteer at hospitals and such."

"Where have you been before?"

The rabbi appeared to become a bit agitated. His answer was gruff. "Actually, I haven't had a congregation in quite some time."

At this point, I interjected, "Excuse me, rabbi. Where else have you volunteered?"

His tone changed noticeably. "Well, around. You know?"

I persisted. "Have you had experience counseling the children of former camp inmates? In Brooklyn, maybe?"

"See here, young man. . . ."

"Schneider, rabbi. Lenny Schneider."

"No need to introduce yourself. I know you very well."

Then, with no further preamble, the rabbi drew a gun. I jumped from the bed with all the speed I could muster, and managed, just, to deflect the pistol. It went off, the bullet smashing into the bedstead a foot from Sol's face.

Sol grabbed the gun hand, and I brought my cast down on Mueller's head. The cast smashed, my arm broadcast pain throughout my body, and Mueller slumped onto Sol's bed. Sol had the gun out of his hand a second later.

Every nurse on the floor was in our room a second after that, faces contorted by shock and fear.

Sol looked at our nurse and said, "Next time, send a priest."

forty-three

THE JOINT WAS JUMPIN'
after that. Cops, hospital administrators, curious patients:
all came and went in a constant swirl of humans. A
doctor reset my re-broken arm amidst the fun.

Special Agent Clarke showed up in about two hours,
and the crowd was turned out. Clarke, accompanied by
another FBI man who looked like his clone, shut the
door.

"Jesus H. Christ, Schneider, you have certainly been
busy. You can't stay out of this even when you're in the
goddamn hospital."

"Don't lose your professional cool, Clarke. I guess
my dance card has been full, but, without me, you'd still
be scratching your ass. Now you've got Farkas and a
bunch of his boys, and Mueller, a war criminal. You
might even get Dorfler. All I get is beat up, and you'll
get a promotion. I'd be happy to trade, except I'd rather
play piano in a whorehouse than work for the Injustice
Department. You got a lot of fuckin' nerve coming in
here and upsetting a couple of sick men. Right, Uncle
Sol?"

"Goddamn right!"

Clarke sighed. "Okay, okay. We're outta here. The Bureau will be in touch to take depositions from you two. Don't worry, it won't be me deposing you. I'd rather spend the rest of my life in the Iowa office."

"Whaddaya got against Iowa?" asked Uncle Sol.

Clarke and his silent shadow left.

"I'd shake hands with you, Uncle Sol, but my arm hurts too much."

"*Momsers*! Commies they found where there weren't any. Once, did they find a Klu Klux who killed anybody? Everybody in the barber shop knew who they were, the FBI couldn't find 'em. Ptui!"

"Let's get some rest. Seamus is bringing some franks for dinner."

"Lenny, your diet will give me permanent heartburn. How are the hot dogs at Yankee Stadium?"

forty-four

Seamus came with his homemade best right around dinner time. Uncle Sol was amused by our vicious banter, and I apologized, yet again, for inadvertently putting him in harm's way. Stuffed and satisfied, we said good night to Feeney the Weenie and crashed.

Sometime later, I felt the softest of touches on my shoulder. So soft it did not startle me awake. I opened my eyes to see the hulking Bruno kneeling at my bedside. Those huge paws could break a man's neck, yet coax delicate, achingly sweet music from a piano. I was glad he was my friend.

"What's up?" I whispered, as Bruno touched his finger to his lips.

"Want out?" Even his whisper rumbled.

"Fuckin' A."

I slipped my legs over the side of the bed, making the plastic sheets crackle. Bruno shot me a reproving look, and I moved more slowly and deliberately. My clothes, the same nasty stuff I had worn during the climactic events of the past week, were rank. I shuddered to put them on again.

As we headed for the door, Uncle Sol raised himself and waved. We waved back.

We exited the hospital down a set of fire stairs. Bruno had rigged the door so that it didn't lock, or set off an alarm either. His Cadillac was parked close by.

The fresh air was marvelous. I was a bit unsteady on my pins, but the sweet air and the first chill of autumn was bracing. We got in the car, and headed toward the highway.

"Thanks for busting me out," I said. "They were probably sick of me in there, anyway."

"You're famous. The word's out that you got ridda Louie Carmine." Bruno looked over at me with a sardonic grin.

"Yeah, well, you and I both know that's bullshit."

Bruno shrugged. "Hey, the world floats on a sea of bullshit."

"So, have you straightened them out?"

"Not my job. Besides, it ain't so bad that they believe that. First of all, this gives you more respect. They really hated the son of a bitch. Second, it opens up more sources for scuttlebutt from the street. They'll be easier with the info because they respect you. Third, I'd rather have the skinheads after you than me or the old man."

"Thanks for nothing. Seriously, Bruno, what about the skinheads? Are they after me?"

"Don't worry about nothin' yet. There's not that many of them left from Carmine's gang, and they're gonna do a stretch at Attica. A couple a' years of makin' license plates and takin' showers with minorities'll get you off their minds. And, if some punk wants to take you on when he gets out, we'll deal with it then.''

"Forgive me if I don't sigh with relief. Rabid skin-heads in my future. I shoulda been a chiropodist.''

"Huh?''

I waved it off. "Never mind.''

An hour after we left the hospital, I was standing in front of my apartment house. It was 2 am. Bruno called at me from the car.

"Yo! Tommy Flanagan is gonna be at the Blue Note. Wanna go?''

"Damn right. Call me, okay?''

"Later.'' He drove off.

Once inside my place, I stripped off the grungy clothes and took a shower, careful to keep my cast outside the curtain. What a pain in the ass. Not only was it my writing hand, but it performed several other functions, all of which I would have to do for a while on the sinister side. I had broken my right hand once before, and didn't look forward to learning to do all this stuff lefty. Then, I realized that I was very lucky to be alive and mostly in one piece.

Once the introspection begins, I can either short-circuit it or go with it. I struggled to open a San Miguel beer, and went with it. Unable to dick around with CD boxes, I put on the jazz station, real soft. There was a lot to think about.

When one is already of a somewhat ambivalent nature, dilemmas are the pits. Especially dilemmas of a moral or existential sort, and I was up to here with them.

First, I had little to do with the resolution of these matters. The dog thing I gave to the cops. I was just a passenger for the finish of the Uncle Sol and Nicky Carmine cases. I had never felt so carried along by events, so . . . ineffectual. Maybe I should stick with stakeouts and file searches. Maybe this Sam Spade stuff ain't what it's cracked up to be. But, then, it's in the job description, don't you know.

And I sure won't go back to waiting tables or doing standup comedy.

Then there was Sue. What the hell? I've just been reminded that, a) she's like a hemorrhoid on the psyche, and b) I often rely on her as a sounding board and source of inspiration. Usually a divorce uncomplicates your relationship in vital ways, absent kids or shared property. Our divorce—if it can really be called a divorce—has jolted our relationship into another plane of existence. We get along better not living under the same roof, our sexual problems are in deep remission, and it's obvious that she still cares, and that I do, too.

The only problem with this marriage is that there isn't one.

Am I falling in love with Mickey? Yeah. I guess. Do I need this? No. I guess. Will it make my life more complicated? Does Groucho have a mustache? Does Monk play in the cracks? Has Pete Rose seen a horse race?

Also, I hadn't come face to face with my Jewishness for a long time. Sure, I know what I am, but I don't identify with the religious or militantly Zionist part of it. Culturally, I'm proud to be part of the people that gave the world Moses and Jesus and Nostradamus and Spinoza and Marx (Karl, Harpo, etc.) and Freud and Einstein and Salk and Mahler and Gershwin and Koufax and Stan Getz and Benny Goodman and Jack Benny and Jerry Lewis.

Whoa. I'd better quit there.

Anyway, on a day-to-day basis, I'm just another guy.
I guess I needed to be reminded that it is far more important to others, in some ways I normally don't think
about. And that old emotions and prejudices I think we
have gotten past are a real, daily component of some
people's lives.

Take Farkas. His parents' nightmares informed his
life. I don't know what he might have been if he had
grown up to typical suburban Jewish life. Whatever it
might have been, he would have excelled. He had the
capacity to involve himself deeply in anything he felt
was important. I have always lacked this quality, and I
envy him. There was a lot of the existential hero in him:
true to his own moral code, and defined by his actions.
I envy him this, also.

I am the opposite of the deeply involved man of action. I sometimes feel that I have never cared passionately about anything, not even my political convictions
in the 60s. Then, I remember that Farkas is as cold-
blooded a killer as I have ever met, as vicious as Kaminsky, in his way. And, each formed and animated by
old hatreds.

I flashed that this whole thing involved revenge, and
the need to get even, or finish up past dirty work. Lou
Goffin needed help because Uncle Sol wanted revenge.
Farkas and his merry men wanted revenge. Nicky
wanted revenge. LeVine wanted to keep his depraved
dream alive.

It is one of those philosophical truisms that revenge
exacts a toll on the carrier, as well as the object, of
vengeful feelings. Sol's life was pickled in his bitterness.
Farkas, intelligent, fearless, and passionate, became a
shark—amoral, implacable, deadly. Nicky was pretty far

gone, anyway, but it's true that his desire to get even was his end.

There's an old saying that revenge is a dish best served cold. Like most old sayings, it has more than a little truth to it. But, revenge is one dish that is quickly re-heated. Even forty years later, it can be served piping hot.

I stuffed some weed into a corn-cob pipe. I smoked myself to sweet oblivion, with Sarah Vaughan singing softly out of my radio.

"It ain't no use for you to cry, cry, cry . . ." she sang. She didn't know the half of it.

forty-five

I WALKED UP THE STAIRS to my office, feeling as decrepit as the building. A couple of days worth of mail wedged under the door preventing access and causing me to stoop down to unjam it. The arm ached inside the cast. I let out an audible groan, and Sister Arletta peeked out her door to see what the noise was.

"It's just me, Arletta."

"Jesus. What the hell happened to you?"

"I thought you psychic types were supposed to know everything. Why don't you wiggle your Ouija and take a guess?"

"Schneider, you won't stop making smartass remarks until three days after you're dead. Really, what happened?"

So, I stood there in the hallway giving her the Reader's Digest version of the past few days. Sometime during my oration, her chief rival and lover, Madame Yvonne, came out to listen. They both made appropriate clucking sounds and inhalations of breath to show their shock and outrage.

My phone rang, and I excused myself. It was Mickey.

"Lenny, I called the hospital and they said you got up and left. Are you nuts, or what?"

"Yeah, maybe. Hospitals make me that way. I feel like I can get better quicker if I don't have to put up with angels of mercy waking me out of a sound sleep to give me a sedative. Besides, they wouldn't let me drink any beer or play loud music."

She sighed. "I suppose you're right. If they really pissed you off you might do something regrettable. Look, I want to meet you for lunch. Can do?"

"I'll tell you what. I've really got to do some paperwork, and I have to line up some jobs for next week. I can't keep living on my vanishing bank account."

"Next week? You are crazy. Okay, I'll pick up something and meet you down there. Any requests?"

"Nothing I can talk about on the phone without violating federal laws. But, you could stop at Katz's and bring me a tongue on club with mustard and sauerkraut, and a kasha knish from Yonah Shimmel's."

"Shimmel is closed. It's Saturday."

"Yeah, right. Okay, a potato nick from Katz's."

"I'll be there in an hour." She rang off.

There was a knock on my door. "Come in," I bellowed.

It was Arletta and Yvonne. One carried a cup of herb tea, the other some kind of large capsule with what looked like leaves ground up in it.

"Drink this tea," said Arletta, "it'll snap back like Stanback."

"And swallow this. It's good for what ails you," said Yvonne, proffering the horse pill.

Resistance was futile. I grimaced and swallowed the pill. The herb tea was delicious.

"Thanks, kids. I appreciate the kindness."

"Just give a yell if you need us. We'll come back for the cup later."

It was odd. I had never seen them work together like that. They had ceased to be rivals and were functioning like two parts of a single entity. It reminded me of the twins in *Lord of the Flies* who were so close they were referred as one being, Samneric. It was kind of sweet.

The answering service came up with a few leads. I made phone calls and got some soft jobs: process serving, the daytime shift on a stakeout, and a few bodyguard assignments I would pass on to Bruno, or one of his ilk. My God, how the money rolls in.

As I was opening the mail, Mickey breezed in with a brown bag showing the tell-tale grease spots of a deli lunch. My doctor once told me that this food has killed more Jews than the Nazis. I wonder if Uncle Sol would agree.

With a minimum of prologue, she laid out the feast. In addition to the food, she had purchased a Dr. Brown's Cel-Ray for herself, and a bottle of Harp lager for me. A beauty? A doll!

We made small talk as we ate. She told me that the softball team had won its game against The Bronx, despite having neither her nor me there. She told me that Uncle Sol was feeling okay, and just today had cried his eyes out over his murdered family, the first time he had permitted himself to do this in nearly 50 years.

Her father, who claimed to have had about six heart attacks in the last few days, was taking time off work, and considering a vacation in Miami Beach. I made a mental note to tell him to go to Joe's for stone crabs, until I remembered that they were still out of season.

Along about the time we were getting to the chocolate-covered halavah for dessert, she said, "Lenny, can I ask you something?"

Uh-oh. "Um, yeah, sure. Anything."

"Well, I've been thinking. I used to be a teacher, you know, in junior high? I haven't really had a job in almost two years. My pop's business gives us enough so it hasn't been a problem. Now, I don't think I could cope with getting back into a room with 35 pubescent delinquents. Sooo, I was wondering. . . ."

"Yeah?"

"How would you like a partner? A Ms. Inside to your Mr. Outside."

About like another 15 rounds with Nicky and the skinheads, I thought. I said, "Jeez, well, I never thought. . . ."

"No, really. I mean, this place is always in a state and you wouldn't even have to pay me and I think that it might be good for both of us and you could get rid of that awful answering service and Mrs. Cohen would get her rent on time and I could handle the paperwork leaving you to. . . ."

"Whoa, Nellie. Mickey, look, I mean, I don't know, what with our, um, relationship and all, and. . . ."

"Oh, come on! Don't be a schmuck. Just try it for a while. All I want is a chance."

I sighed. "And if it really doesn't work I could come to you and discuss it calmly?"

"Yup."

"And no recriminations, or consequences for us. You know what I mean, 'us'?"

"Yup. I promise." She crossed her heart elaborately. I sighed again. "I gotta be crazy, but, okay."

She actually jumped up and down and squealed like a teenager. Then, Sue walked in. She looked at Mickey, she glowered at me. I wondered how much worse it would hurt if I threw myself out of the window.

Sue drawled, "Hey, Lenny. Who's Raggedy Ann here?"

Thinking fast, I said, "Uh, Sue, this is Mickey. Mickey, meet Sue, my, um . . ."

"Wife," Sue said, in her best Bowie-knife voice.

"Uh, ex-wife, actually," I added lamely.

Mickey straightened up, and said, with immense dignity, "Oh, yes. Lenny has told me so much about you. Isn't it nice that you are able to remain acquainted after, well, everything. It certainly is a tribute to Lenny."

I could feel the blood draining from my head. Suddenly, 15 rounds with Nicky seemed like a trip to Miami Beach. I made pathetic attempts to speak.

Sue looked at Mickey. I will swear that I saw venom drip from her teeth.

"Well, Lenny, I came by because I heard from Bruno. He told me you were out of the hospital. I rushed right over, but that was before I knew that you had Anne of Green Gables here to mop your fevered brow."

"Actually, my name is Melanie. My friends call me Mickey. You can call me Mrs. Adler."

"You can't even imagine what I'll call you, you—"

"Hold it!" I yelled, so hard that it hurt me. "Believe it or not, I really am bent up and this is not helping me one bit. Now, I know this is probably not the best way for you to have met"—my funeral being the best, I thought—"but that is no excuse for the two of you to behave like this. Okay?"

Sue snarled. Mickey grumbled.

"I'll call you later," Sue spit. She did a 180, and went out the door. I caught a glimpse of Arletta, Yvonne, and Feinbaum's painted scalp as the door swung shut. Sue sounded like a herd of rhino going down the stairs, except that rhino don't talk like that. Lifers in maximum security prisons don't talk like that.

Mickey turned to me and smiled about 107% too sweetly. "Nice outfit. Too bad about the rest."

"Will you be starting tomorrow, Mrs. Adler?"

Mickey snapped to attention. "Yes, sir! And, please," she cooed, sprawling over my desk, "call me 'Raggedy Ann.' "

"See you about 9:30."

She blew me a kiss, and walked out.

I sat silent, brooding, for about ten minutes. Then, I hauled myself up, walked to the door, and yelled out into the hallway, "Yvonne? You got another pill?"